T0195733

A Good Girl's Journal
of
Dirty Little Secrets

Zoey Truth

authorHOUSE®

AuthorHouse™
1663 Liberty Drive
Bloomington, IN 47403
www.authorhouse.com
Phone: 1 (800) 839-8640

Published by AuthorHouse 01/23/2015

ISBN: 978-1-4969-6395-6 (sc)
ISBN: 978-1-4969-6396-3 (hc)
ISBN: 978-1-4969-6394-9 (e)

Library of Congress Control Number: 2015900748

Acknowledgment

I would like to thank my mom for designing the cover and pretending like she isn't freaked out about what's inside of this book.

You're the best mom in the whole world.

I would also like to thank Daphne Oxford, my best friend and the woman who is like a sister to me. Thank you for pushing me to get this book done then taking the time to read and critique every word.

A very special thank you to my very special friend who has been inspiring me for a very long time. I don't even need to say your name. You know who you are . . . my real life "kryptonite."

And thank you to all of my brothers, sisters and sister in-law for your undying support and encouragement.

Sister in-law I promise we'll go on that big family vacation like you want.

A big thank you to all of my friends who have listened to me, encouraged me and shown me nothing but love and support as I worked to realize a dream.

All My Love,
Zoey Truth

Journal Entries

Prologue

I was always the good girl growing up, the teacher's pet, and the one who did the right thing most of the time. I grew up in church and that meant my parents had strict rules. There was no sex, no staying out late, and definitely no talking back.

I was the one who definitely did what my parents said to a "T." I graduated and went off to college an inexperienced, naive young girl.

Sure, I'd done a lot of personal exploring and experimenting with my body. Kissed a few boys of course, and let a few cop a feel of my breasts and booty every now and then, but that was the extent of my experience.

My first year of college changed all of that.

One of the things I learned about myself is: it's okay to love who you are and love to have fun with yourself and others. I learned to stop apologizing for my sex appeal and love of the orgasm. Once I freed myself from the chokehold of public opinion, I was free to really enjoy my life.

So who am I? I am an average career woman with an appetite for fun. I am like most women when it comes to being intimate with someone. I want the passion, closeness, and friendship. I want to get the most out of life, I want to feel good, and I don't want to be judged for doing what comes naturally to most human beings. I want to live my fantasies.

I love that people have no idea I indulge my freaky side when I say yes to sneaking off from work for a little X-rated fun or waking up and having the man I'm with for breakfast. It's fun living the secret life. Public me is by no means as innocent as I used to be, but you can't tell what I'm really into just by listening to me talk or watching me walk. (Well, you may be able to sense hints of my freakiness when you see my hips sway, but the depth of my insatiable thirst for getting it on is unimaginable.)

While we may not admit it to ourselves or others, we all have urges, curiosities, and lust for the forbidden. I'm pulling back the curtain. Welcome to my dirty little secrets.

The touch of a hand brushing across your skin awakens every nerve in your body.

The first time you have that feeling is liberating; it gives you a rollercoaster rush.

It's a feeling everyone only gets to experience once, so you might as well make the most of it.

Baby Steps

It was the middle of summer. I was thirteen, and hanging out in my room. Like most teenagers, I was curious about sex, and this different kind of book I was reading gave me a peek inside of this forbidden world.

Sicily, my best friend at the time, gave me this very special "grown up" book.

It was called "*Lucky*," by Jackie Collins, and little did I know it was about to make me a lucky girl.

I read stuff in that book that made me feel things I'd never felt before.

Up until that point, I had barely looked at myself naked, and only touched myself out of necessity, not pleasure. I didn't always appreciate my shape. Like any teen, there were times when I was very much ashamed of how curvy and imperfect my body was. I wasn't skinny, but I wasn't fat—I just wasn't properly proportioned.

Everything changed the summer I read that book.

The men and women in that book did things to each other I couldn't even imagine doing to another person.

They kissed each other in places I never touched; their hands were constantly roaming over each other's bodies.

They did more than just drink the alcohol—they used it as basting before licking every inch of skin available to them.

They made love anywhere and everywhere, unabashed. Have mercy, what the hell was going on here?

Reading and imagining all of what was happening on those pages awakened my insides. I had no idea what was happening. I was a church girl, for goodness sake; we didn't even talk about things like this.

I would read and notice my thighs rubbing together. I had urges, but at that time I didn't know they were urges.

I knew that whatever I was feeling, it was making a mess in my panties.

I wanted to do what the characters in this book were doing. Men were opening the legs of women and sticking their fingers inside of them, they were rubbing their clits . . . I wasn't even 100 percent sure I knew what a clit was, but I knew where those parts were on my body, and knew there was no reason my fingers couldn't find their way down there. I didn't know what was going to happen. I knew it felt like I peed and didn't wipe, and it was slippery.

I thought I would want to stop, but I didn't.

I rubbed around, soft and slow at first, just to see how I would feel. Then I went faster and harder; it felt so good. I didn't want to stop, and couldn't stop, even if I wanted to. Things were happening: my breathing was changing, it was faster and deeper. My fingers were working overtime.

Then I felt this strange sensation roll through my entire body. It made me tense up, and when I relaxed I could hear myself making this noise—it was a moan mixed with a small squeal. I wasn't expecting that, and I was worried one of my brothers or sisters would hear me. My heart was pounding, my hand was shaking a little.

It was the first time I'd masturbated, and it felt good. It's also where I developed my appetite for orgasms, and I was starving.

To this day I still relish my wetness, and let's just say I still hold a sweet spot for my sweet spot.

I have some very fond, vivid memories from my college days. It's where I learned to give and receive. When you go from having an intimate relationship with yourself to sharing your body with an actual human being, there is a lot to take in. I am thankful I was such an avid reader because it gave me a leg up. So what is a girl to do when she's faced with something she's never done before? She wings it.

It's About Time

So this was really about to happen. I was about to give it up for the first time. I'm not sure what I thought it was going to be like; perhaps I thought it was going to be more of a movie like setup.

The magical moment was going to happen after we looked longingly and lovingly into each other's eyes. YEAH, NOT SO MUCH.

In reality, I was with a horny man-child named Terrance who already had more sexual experiences than I'd come close to dreaming about.

He was a man with a captivating smile and a boyish charm, so it was easy to see how a woman could be spellbound.

Terrance had smooth, dark brown skin. His voice was just slightly hypnotic, or maybe it was just new to my ears because of all I didn't know.

I came from the type of home where my parents kept a close eye on us. We weren't getting out of the house long enough to do any real damage; all we had were our fantasies, which is why I thought my first time was going to be fantastic.

Terrance and I were in my dorm room. I'd held out for a couple of months because I thought that's what you were supposed to do. He spent many a night trying to convince me to give it up using his body, and what a body it was.

I thought he was too young to have such a chiseled body. None of the other new college athletes were as built as he was, at least not in my mind. He had these great arm muscles and strong legs to go along with his handsome, disarming face, but he wasn't much of a smooth talker. That's probably why we were just sitting in my room at 10 o'clock at night. This night I guess I was just a little anxious to see what all the sex hoopla was about. Unlike in the movies, there was no romantic gaze; in fact, this fool had this sense of entitlement about getting the goods. He was acting like because he was in my room after sundown, he was supposed to get into my panties.

Fortunately for him, I didn't care, because I was wet and curious myself.

It was awkward. I was sitting on the bed with my shirt and panties on, because I wasn't ready for him to see my whole body. I was still a bit self-conscious—not that he noticed, he was only interested in trying to get inside.

He was kissing me, which was easy enough, and he was rubbing on my body. I didn't know what the hell to do, so I just let him take the lead.

Then I remembered something I read in one of my many "grown up" books, I reached down and undid his pants so I could touch it, the thing that would be going inside of me soon. I felt all clumsy, again something he didn't seem to notice. For all of his experience, he was still an extra-horny teenager, just like me.

The kissing was getting more intense, then he went for my shirt. He wanted to lift it over my head. I didn't want it off yet but I didn't try to stop it, plus it was dark inside of my room so I didn't think he could see much. My heart was pounding. I was worried he could feel it or see it beating through my chest.

All I could think was, please don't let me mess this up, please don't let this man find out I'm a virgin.

I had to be good, didn't I?

He unclasped my bra and I nervously shimmied out of it, then he did something that would become my favorite act of intimacy of all time: he sucked my nipples. The feeling I had was almost indescribable. I felt tingly. I felt my body move in closer to his; it was like I was now a spectator. Everything seemed to be happening without any assistance from me. I wanted more of whatever this feeling was.

I'd touched myself a lot over the last few years, but this was different. My juices were flowing, my panties were very wet.

Next thing I knew, he was lying me down and pulling off my underwear.

This was it, I was about to give up my virginity. I was ready for it to happen, I willed it to happen.

He used his fingers to play around down there. I wasn't sure what was supposed to be happening. I'm pretty sure it was supposed to feel good, but I was too nervous to really get the full effect. At that point, I was ready for the main show. I needed it to just be over so I could say I'd done it and find out if he could make me feel as good as I made myself feel. I wasn't sure if I was supposed to make noise, but noise involuntarily came from my lips the longer he kept his fingers inside of me.

Then he took off his clothes, giving me a good look at the outline of his physique. It was dark so I couldn't see all of the detail, but as I said before, he was an athlete, a very in-shape football player standing in front of me, the former fat chick whose body was finally taking shape. He wanted me at that moment, and I was all too happy to make sure he had me.

It was as if he was reading my mind. It seemed as if he stood there for a few extra seconds to let me take it all in before putting his body over mine.

I didn't know much, but I knew enough to ask him to put a condom on before we were too far gone. This was one good girl who wasn't going to end up with a baby the first time out of the gate.

He obliged, but at that point he would've agreed to anything to get what he wanted from me. Okay, now back to the matter at hand. He put himself inside of me. It hurt a little, but since I was faking like I wasn't a virgin, I sucked in my breath. When I look back on it now, I think he interpreted this action as him being so big he was filling me up, but there was some closet space left.

I knew what to do instinctively. I knew to rotate my hips, I knew I needed to hold on to him—he was nice to hold anyway, remember? . . . the great body.

I was gyrating, he was pumping, I was sweating, I didn't know what was really happening. I just kept thinking, I'm officially not a virgin anymore.

I don't know how long it all lasted. I remember him cumming, but I didn't. I knew what an orgasm felt like from the hundreds of times I'd masturbated, and I know I didn't feel that just then, but I did feel a sense of freedom. I had finally done "IT" and I was glad I did, even if it wasn't like I dreamed it would be.

Once he released, he kind of just collapsed on top of me and went to sleep. Yes, he went to sleep right on top of me, still inside of me. I couldn't move.

I just lay there wondering how long this little nap was going to last. Was he drooling on me? Yes he was. I couldn't help but smile because I felt like, damn, I did a good job on my first time in the saddle.

Or was he just exhausted from hours of trying to talk me into doing the deed?

People play games. It's human nature. It's how we learned to talk, walk, and break the ice. So why wouldn't you play the same games when it came to getting intimate with someone? When a boy liked you, he would come up to you, push or hit you, and run.

Why would getting someone in the bed be any different?

Full Contact Sport

There was this guy I met in college. He was kinda cute—okay, very cute. I didn't know I wanted him until I actually had him.

His name was Jayson.

I'd seen him around campus and knew he liked to show off a little. He clearly liked to be noticed and I noticed; however, I didn't know if he noticed me noticing. One day I found out he did know I was watching him. We didn't really meet until we started working together at the gym.

The first day all of the new employees were gathered in a room, I spotted him and waved; he waved back. It was at that moment I knew something was going to happen between us. I wasn't sure why I knew it, but it was the feeling I got when we looked at each other. They say women know immediately whom they're going to sleep with, and maybe that's what I was feeling.

I was going to give it to him, and I'm pretty sure my body language told him all he needed to know.

I smiled and unconsciously, (or maybe it was consciously, who knows), thrust my breasts out just enough for him to see there was definitely a body there to be desired. I didn't think he picked up on by subtle cues until after the big meeting ended. He came over and offered me a ride.

Well it would've been easy to say yes, but why make things easy?

I was about the chase. I loved to chase and loved being chased. Would this be a sprint or marathon? I wasn't sure yet, so I passed on the ride.

We had some small talk and I walked away, making sure to put an extra little something in my step for him to watch, even though my booty already had a rhythm of its own. I didn't know how this was going to play out; I wasn't even sure I was going to be spending any time with him.

Fast-forward two weeks when we ended up overlapping on a Friday shift. This was almost too perfect.

I was getting off, and he was coming on the clock.

Now what? There was no way I could leave, but I couldn't just hang around "chatting." I had to quickly figure out a way to waste time without being obvious.

I always kept my gym clothes with me when I worked, just in case I felt like working out. Today it was going to pay off.

I changed into my workout gear and sweat it out for about an hour.

Here's where it all got tricky. He had at least another hour of work. I had to find a way to linger inconspicuously. I went back behind the counter for my things. It just so happened my gym attire didn't leave much to the imagination.

It was a shorts unitard that was of course very revealing; as I said, I had a great body.

I had curves and a flat belly—it was easy. I had to pretend to have some sense of humility, so I wore a T-shirt over the outfit, but all that did was make my booty look a lot hotter and juicier. I methodically walked over by him to drop my towel in the bin.

He asked me if I was about to leave. I said yep, but I was thinking, if you say the right words, I'll stay.

He asked what I was about to do. I answered, I was going to take a shower and grab something to eat.

I still hadn't sat down in one of the two seats at the counter where the staff on duty checked in members and gave them towels.

Then he made the move that would change our relationship: he asked me to watch the counter while he ran to the restroom. Bingo!

I sat down and made myself comfortable, and when he got back we talked. The banter was effortless, the electricity was obvious.

Somehow we ended up talking about cooking. I bragged about how I could throw down in the kitchen. He said he was hungry. I was too, and I offered to cook for him, a man who was virtually a stranger.

His shift was ending so he offered me a ride home for a second time.

This time I took him up on the offer. He'd been checking me out throughout the entire conversation, and I made sure I gave him plenty to look at, too.

I leaned in at times so he could see me stretch; it was a subliminal message to let him know I could stretch out in bed. I got up a few times pretending I was leaving so he could get an eyeful of all of my ass being hugged by that skintight workout suit. I knew it was inappropriate but I didn't care, I was in high flirt mode.

I felt a sense of accomplishment as we walked out the door and down the stairs of the gym. I got into his car and made myself comfortable, but of course I was nervous. I didn't know what was going to happen that night. By the time I'd met him I'd only been with two other guys, but hey, I was going to see where this little flirt led me. Even though the offer was to drop me off at my place, we passed where I lived. We ended up at his apartment. He turned on the TV, and I sat there while he showered. I was still a sweaty mess from working out, but I guess that didn't matter to him or me. I asked him what he wanted me to cook. He pulled out some microwavable meal. I was thinking, what is this? How am I supposed to cook this?

He went back to his bedroom to actually get in the shower this time. When he came back, the bottom half of his dark chocolate body was wrapped in a towel. I tried not to look directly at him. I was there to cook, right?

He went back to that tired looking TV dinner. I kept thinking, where is the food he wants me to cook? I was clearly very naive because I thought I was seducing him, but he had the upper hand and I didn't even realize it.

He walked back into his bedroom and asked me to come in there.

I was a little timid all of a sudden because he called me back to his room.

He told me to sit down. I wasn't sure about this, but I did it anyway, what happened next was a little shocking.

He grabbed me but he didn't kiss me, so naturally I wanted to get out of his grasp.

This led to some strange wrestling match. I'm competitive by nature, so of course I was going to hold my own. It was weird, but I found myself getting turned on by this, and I wasn't sure why.

He wasn't necessarily grabbing any of the vital private parts, like my breasts and pussy. It was the force he was using on me— it wasn't too hard, just enough to offer resistance to fight against.

The harder I fought, the more I was turned on.

Then he tried to pull my shirt off, and that's when I tried to stop him. I was still sweaty; I told him we shouldn't do it tonight. He played dumb, asking, "Do what?"

I didn't answer him, mostly because his mouth was over mine. Now he was rubbing my body.

He too was turned on by our bodies clashing. His towel had come off, and that's when I saw how much he was packing. Suddenly I forgot I was supposed to be saying no to this weird foreplay we were engaged in.

I was distracted long enough for him to flip me over and slap my ass.

That snapped me back into reality. I began the struggle to get up, saying, "Hey, I have to go, I'm all sweaty, let me shower and we can do this another time."

He didn't say anything, he just kept wrestling. I couldn't figure out why I liked this game so much, but I was so hot and bothered at this point.

My legs seemed to be opening involuntarily. I was losing control of myself, and wouldn't you know it, he'd managed to get the straps of my clothes off my shoulders. I kind of liked that I was losing this battle, but I was going to keep fighting the good fight; that is, until he pulled the unitard all the way down.

I was not wearing any underwear, so once the shorts were down, they were down. My legs were open and I was exposed.

He pinned my hands above my head. Okay, so is this the part where I give up?

Of course not. Well, not until he started kissing me and biting my bottom lip.

So okay, I'm going to give up, because quite frankly I'm just too weak to keep up the charade.

I took a deep breath and decided it was definitely going to happen. I was going to give it up for sure.

Oh wait! As I was thinking this, I felt him sliding inside of me. I arched my back because I wanted to give him clearance to give me all he had. He picked up on my unspoken "yes" to his body joining with mine, and he settled himself inside of me—well, as settled as two people can get while getting it on.

I knew he was sexy, and I had just discovered he was packing, and jackpot! He was talented. I still tried to resist a little, but any time I did, he pulled my arms over my head and looked me in the eyes as he drilled deeper inside of me. He was basically rendering me immobile, leaving me only able to take the punishment his dick gave my pussy, and it was what I needed. I loved it. He was a new experience.

I tried to get in on the game by wrapping my legs around him, hoping to get some leverage, but all it did was cause him to flip me over, where he proceeded to nibble on my neck. Oh boy, I didn't want that, I didn't want any marks. "No marks," I whispered. So he proceeded to kiss my body from the neck down. He pushed my face down toward the mattress. I wasn't really sure of what was going on at this time, I was just pretending to know bed tricks.

He positioned my well-toned ass where he wanted it to be before pushing back inside of me.

He held onto me tight and hit it hard from the back. I don't know what made me say this in the middle of all of this romping, but I said, "Hey, we should stop."

I shocked myself. I don't think he blinked—not that I would've been able to see if he did since he was behind me. He simply replied, "Do you really want me to stop?"

Well, of course I didn't want him to stop; even as I was saying no, I was trying to push myself against him.

Me saying no seemed to only make him go harder.

He turned me back over again. I tried to get out of the bed again—for what, I don't know. I guess I was just trying to keep this fun, weird, sort of no/yes, no/yes thing going. He pulled me back down with just enough force to put me on my back. He kissed me hard. I felt the force of his tongue making me hungrier for him. My sexy new coworker pulled my legs up and opened them wide.

He was on his knees pumping inside of me. I didn't even know my legs could spread that wide.

The feeling was so good, better than I'd felt before, but I didn't know how to release it. I was too overwhelmed and too self-conscious to let it go, so I rocked with him until he came. Right after that he spanked me on my ass and he got in the shower, leaving me there to figure out what just happened.

After that, he ordered pizza, we ate, and I fell asleep. The next day he dropped me off and I slinked back to my dorm room like the hussy I was . . . HA!

There is nothing wrong with being nice in order to spare the feelings of others. It's okay to be kind when you think the person is just having an off day, and he or she may be worthy of a second chance. But what about when the person is so awful that you don't want to ever go there again? Sometimes being nice isn't all it's cracked up to be, trust me.

Faking It: A Cautionary Tale

I didn't know any better. I thought it was what nice people did to keep from hurting the feelings of other nice people.

I stayed on campus that summer to take a few classes along with Reggie, this fairly nice-looking guy in town for the summer. He wasn't the finest man I'd ever met. His body was kind of soft, but not mushy.

But truth be told, I didn't mind a little pudge in the middle; sometimes I found it to be slightly sexy.

Reggie was cool. We hit it off rather quickly, joking around with each other at first, playing the familiar cat-and-mouse game horny people play to see if the other is interested. He was definitely interested, as was I.

I've always been a rather aggressive woman, not one for wasting time while someone gets comfortable enough to ask me out or ask me for something else. I made the first move by teaming up with him on a class project.

It was one I could do in my sleep, so I didn't have to concentrate too hard on it. I just needed some play time.

Yes, yes, I know I was there to learn, blah, blah, blah, but college was a time for exploring and having a little fun too.

The next day I came to class in shorts that were just short enough to be appropriate. I have great legs: they're thick, strong, smooth, and look great on someone's shoulders. Oh, did I mention they were attached to the greatest, firmest, roundest booty? I knew Reggie wouldn't be able to turn away from it—plus, my tank top was hugging my double Ds and the girls were sitting up nicely. (Hey, I was in college! Everything sat in place without much provocation.)

I sat down and leaned to the side.

I watched as his eyes took in my entire body, from my platform sandals to my dark brown lipstick up to my braids.

He looked like he wanted to take me down right then and there. Instead, all he could muster was, "You look nice."

That's it? That's the best he had for me? I thought.

Oh boy, this was going to be harder than I thought. We were starting with baby steps, but we only had a few weeks in class, so we really needed to get the lead out. "Thanks," I said, sitting up, already bored with this conquest attempt, until I heard him say under his breath, "I could tear that up." Ahhh, there we go.

I smiled a little, more to myself than to him. The game was back on. I didn't let him know I heard him.

It was time to move in. He was sitting at his desk when I walked up behind him to make my move. I leaned over, and put my mouth just close enough to his ear for him to hear me ask what he thought he could do to me.

He turned around. He was eye level with my breasts. His mouth opened, but no words came out.

When he remembered he had a voice, he told me he could make me weak, make me say his name, and make me do whatever he wanted me to do.

"And just how do you plan to do that?"

He shocked me by cupping my left booty cheek and tracing a trail down my thigh. It made me tingle a bit.

Then he started talking about how good he was in bed and how he'd never had anyone tell him he didn't put it down.

So, of course, I invited him over later that afternoon. I told my roommate I was having company, so she said she'd stay in the bedroom of our one-bedroom summer apartment. I didn't have to work that day, so I had plenty of time to play.

I told him to come over in two hours to give myself time to jump in the shower. When he showed up, I answered the door in a T-shirt and lace panties. I didn't want to waste any time talking; he was there for a reason, and that was to service me, not to go over flashcards. Of course, he asked me if I wanted to talk.

Short answer: no, 1 didn't want to talk. I wanted to see if he was as good as he thought he was.

Why did he want to waste time talking?

It's not like we were looking to be booed up. He was only here for a couple of months. I was beginning to think this was a big mistake.

I decided to just kiss him.

We made out like teenagers, getting all hot and bothered. I sat across his lap on the couch, he had his hand up my shirt fondling my breast. I was grinding on him, and was ready to go.

I got up and took off my shirt and sat down on the floor with my legs spread in front of me, trying to give him the nonverbal cue to get naked.

He got the hint and stripped down to his boxers and got on his knees. He licked my breasts as I wrapped my legs around his waist. Yes, it was about to be on for sure.

Of course, he didn't bring any condoms. Luckily, I kept some around. "Take these off," I whispered in his ear, pointing at his boxers.

He did as I requested, but almost immediately I regretted it and wished we could've continued to dry hump like virgins.

I watched him put the condom on, because for some reason I liked watching guys put them on. In this case, I wish I could turn back the clock to avoid seeing all the space left in that rubber. I thought, hmmm, he's not hard yet. To my horror, he was in fact hard—he was just very small. Oh no, I thought, what was I going to do now?

I let this man come over here, and I wasn't going to be able to do anything with him. I had to go through with it. He turned to me as I tried to hide my shock and embarrassment for him. He laid me down and he was in, I think—I mean, he was moving around like he was. I figured, I guess this is my cue. I started moving too and making all kinds of noise that would under normal circumstances mean I was enjoying myself.

Truthfully, I wasn't even sure he was inside of me—I was only hoping he was so I didn't seem crazy. How much longer was this going to last? I wondered. This was awful.

I was writhing around on the floor, giving the performance of my life. Finally, he ended this torture and came. (I mean, I think he did, who knows.) All I was thinking was, this was last call. He didn't have to go home, but he had to get the hell out of here—or at least out of me. He was a sweaty mess on top of me. Normally I didn't mind the sweat—in fact, I loved a good sloppy sex session—but this time it was annoying and disgusting.

I looked up at him and smiled as he talked about how good it was. I thought to myself, yeah, I was good. A good actress! You, well, you—I'm not even sure what you did. I felt I should've been paid for services rendered in this case.

I went to get towels to wipe the disappointment off my body. Wouldn't you know it, that "fool man" looked at me and said, "Do you want to do it again?"

Really? Really? Really?

No, I don't want to do it again, I said to myself, but aloud I said, "Yeah, let's go."

How did this happen? Why did I fake liking it so much? Now I have to get back on the floor and . . . take two.

Before we started, he asked if I wanted to get on top. Was he crazy?

No, I couldn't get on top, because if for some reason he wasn't in there, I wouldn't know. Then he'd know for sure I was screaming, whooping, and hollering for nothing. I simply said, "No, I don't like to ride, I'm sorry." Liar! I thought to myself. I actually loved being on top. I had my best orgasms on top looking down at the man as I rocked on top of him or as he sucked my nipples. I loved it.

Today was not one of those days. I started my fake moaning and "yeah babying" again. Thankfully, it didn't last as long as the first time.

I told him I needed to get ready for work. I offered to let him shower. (I was too nice.)

He took me up on the offer. I peeked in the bedroom at my friend, and she smiled. So did I—but for a different reason.

When he left, I showered, then went to talk to my best friend.

She said that it must've been good. "You were making all kinds of noise."

I replied, "It was the worst sex I've ever had," and explained that because I faked it, I had to do it twice. Then I told her about the bait and switch I just experienced.

After the ordeal, I adopted a new rule: no more faking it!

A tickle from a stranger. A kiss from someone standing in the shadows. An embrace from the one you love.

It all takes you over the edge to a place you've never been before. A place where fetishes and fantasies collide.

The Other Side

I've been to the other side, and I can't say I hated it. In fact, it was quite thrilling.

I was a little nervous because I'd never done anything like that before, but I wasn't going to be the one to back out of the deal.

It was going to be a magical night, one that made me giddy.

I spent the afternoon getting myself ready for the whole experience by looking in the mirror at my naked body. I went over every curve, because they were going to be on display that night. I touched myself the way I thought I would be touched that night.

I started by licking my index finger. It was a light lick, only using the tip of my tongue. I let that finger graze my bottom lip.

I used that same finger to run down my chin, my neck, and between my breasts.

I cupped my breasts and massaged them. I let my thumbs run over my nipples, and they immediately perked up.

I couldn't resist twisting them just a little; it sent a chill down my neck.

I let my hand travel a little farther down my body until I reached my sweet spot. It was smooth and bare, the way I liked it; the way I thought everyone would like it. Now, the challenge was not going inside with the hand I'd been using to explore myself—I needed to save every drop of sugar for later.

Tonight was going to be hot, I thought. Tonight I was going to be a seductress.

I was going to pretend I wasn't scared out of my mind to swim in uncharted waters.

Just in case I couldn't pull this off, I made sure there was plenty of alcohol.

I'd never been with a woman before, but I was excited for this to be my first encounter, and I was going to live out a fantasy I'd had for a while.

It was going down tonight with my man, two other guys, and two women.

Instead of going to the club, we were going to ring in the New Year in a hot sweaty heap on the bed—or any other place we landed.

No, I'm not a lesbian, and I'm not even bisexual. However, I find women beautiful. I like the shape of an ass in jeans. I love how their breasts bounce in tight shirts with buttons that can barely contain what's underneath.

It's sensual, it's sexy, it turns me on, and it makes me want to spread my legs wide for my man.

I dare any woman to say she doesn't find other women sexy, to say she's not the slightest bit aroused at the sight of a switch in tight pants, or slacks that hang over a juicy booty . . . but I digress.

This night was going to be spectacular, and the party was about to begin.

They were cute. One was thick and nicely built, almost an hour glass. The other was short and a freak; she actually brought a collar with a chain. I felt like Cameo's "She's Strange" should've been playing.

I was clearly the only novice in the group. It seemed like I blinked and everyone was naked. Now I was playing catch-up.

I slowly took off my clothes—the little I had on. I purposely wore the shortest shorts I could find, without any underwear, and tank top that hugged me tight enough to allow me to forgo the bra. It was now or never.

The next minute was a blur. When I finally refocused, I felt hands caressing my body. I felt like I was floating—the touches were so light—then each lady took a nipple into her mouth. It was better than I imagined it would be. It felt the way it did when I sucked my own nipple for my man: it sent tingles through my entire body.

Every time I got used to one feeling, another more fabulous one replaced it. This time the feeling was inside my pussy, where the short one was licking. Oh boy!

I felt the urge to explode. I didn't want to be the first one to release, but the way she was pulling at my clit with her lips . . . I was about to lose control. The way the other bit down on my nipple and pulled made me want to scream out with pleasure, which is what I did.

I felt like I was high—or should I say higher—because I'm pretty sure I was high when I started.

My senses were alive. Every touch, every lick, and every tug made me wetter, wetter than I ever remember being.

I wondered if it was too wet down there. Was she enjoying herself as much as I was? Did I even care if she liked it? I felt so good.

At that point, I figured I would let go of the river of passion inside of me because I knew there was plenty more where that came from. I was going to be one up on everyone else, but I would return the favor.

For round one, the boys just watched. Round two would be all theirs.

Most of us have someone that makes us weak, makes us question our sanity.

It's the person that turns your brain to mush.

You would do anything for this person, because breathing the same air renders you useless.

It's a special relationship that's not defined by labels of tradition. Your bond is not dictated by what is considered "normal" by societal standards.

But whenever fate allows you to come together, you make the best of it by making each other beg for mercy.

Kryptonite

His soft lips send electricity through my body every time they meet mine.

Actually, he doesn't even have to touch me. All he has to do is be near me. My body only has to sense his, and I feel the fire of desire flow through me. This is how I feel whenever I'm around kryptonite.

No, I don't mean the green rock that rendered Superman powerless. I mean a tall, dark, chocolate man with a velvety voice that makes me dissolve into a liquid heap of passion.

I'm pretty sure every woman reading this knows what it feels like to be with someone who makes you need to instantly change your panties. It doesn't matter if you're with someone else. This person has your sex number. This person only has to say the word and you fall under his spell. You don't care if you cheat; in fact, you find excuses to justify what you're doing behind the back of your significant other.

I've known my kryptonite for nearly twenty years.

The first night we spent together we were like animals in heat.

We waited two years to intertwine our bodies, and we were tangled the whole night. We conquered each other at least three times before passing out in his bed. I was in college, and back then it was called "creeping." With the sun coming up, it was time for me to creep up out of there, but I was hooked; I knew I had to have more no matter where he was. I knew he wanted me in the same way. What makes kryptonite so irresistible?

In my case, it's the way he looks at me as if he is already tasting me. It's the way he slides in close to my body, as if he stalked me like a lion going after his prey in the jungle.

It's how he orders me to "come here" when he's ready for me; the way he takes off my shirt and liberates my breasts from my bra; and the way he sucks my nipples until he brings me to the brink of orgasm, making me want to beg— but my pride won't let me.

It's the way he lays me down and stares into my eyes before he kisses me, causing me to melt, causing my juices to flow freely. It's how he uses his fingers to slip inside of me, tease me, and make me taste myself before he slips his dick inside of me.

He talks dirty to me; tells me to give it to him while he pulls my hair and makes me bow to his will, doggy style. It's how he makes me moan and shiver with satisfaction as he spanks my ass.

It's how he holds on to me as I cum, making sure I feel the intensity. It's the way he waits for me to get mine before he releases.

I can call my kryptonite whenever I need him. He's my friend with 401(k) benefits. I can't be with him long-term because our passion is too combustible; others are turned on by the heat we generate.

I recently saw my kryptonite, and we didn't jump each other's bones. We hugged, and he gently kissed my lips. He slipped his tongue inside my mouth and caressed my soul. I was breathless.

We didn't go all the way because I brought along the only thing that protects me from the power of kryptonite: a kid with a big mouth.

As I said before, kryptonite is the only thing that can render the Man of Steel virtually useless. It can also bring a superwoman to her knees. (Now, what she does when she gets down there, well . . . let's just say that's what makes me *his* kryptonite.)

We've all run into one before—someone who can't hit the right spot if he had a GPS. You always wonder how this man was able to get more than one woman in the bed. How is it that you'd never heard about this pitiful display of prowess? Who failed at delivering the proper BDR (bad dick report)? Now you gotta deal with this fool.

Bad Dick:
A Dish Best Left Unserved

So I found out the hard way: there is such a thing as really bad dick.

I ran into some bad dick, and like a bad dish, I actually tried it a couple of times to make sure it was nasty.

Everything started off well enough. I met Ray randomly doing a project for work. He seemed nice enough, and he was cute enough, so I gave him my number when he asked. He of course called the same night, and we figured we would grab drinks.

Nothing happened the first night because I just didn't have time, I had to be at work early the next day.

The next time we got together I met him at his place. We sat on the porch with his roommate for a little bit of talking. I had on a sundress that was see-through in direct sunlight. I didn't mind; I was sending a very clear message. I wanted him to know I wasn't wearing any underwear and there was no barrier between his dick and my pussy.

I turned around so Ray could get a good look at my backside. There was a great curve back there; I was just reminding him.

I saw him whisper to his friend, then he escorted me inside to his room.

I was excited to try out this new flavor. He was of course a delicious shade of dark brown with smooth skin. He was a little shorter than I was used to, but hey, why not, I thought. He was kind of sexy.

We only kissed for a little bit, because he was not a candidate for kissing. There was no passion, and we were never able to sync up. Instead, I reached for his pants, because it was time to get down to business. I was going to go down on him and really get him revved up so we could rock it.

I licked him slowly, trying to make him rise to the occasion. I knew I was giving him a great blow job; I could tell by the way he was moving himself inside of my mouth. He wanted to let loose, so I slowed it down a bit because I wanted a chance to let him fill me up first.

I got up off of my knees and undressed slowly for him. There wasn't much to take off, so why not drag out dropping the dress and removing the bra? I was happily exposed, waiting to lead him to the next phase of this trial run.

He was lying back on the bed, so I straddled him and helped him understand he could unlock every emotion with a simple flick of his tongue on my mini mountain peaks. Well, it seemed he was kind of slow and selfish, because all he cared about was making sure he kept getting his. My sexual GPS showed me where this was going: straight down Disappointment Lane.

He put me on my back, effectively ending the foreplay we barely started.

He managed to find the hole and slide in his dick. It started out pretty good. I was feeling good, and he was feeling good inside of me. Then, things went terribly wrong. He started grunting, and I was thinking, oh come on, there is no way this was about to be over already. I'd barely gotten up to 40 miles per hour on my road to the summit and he was already in fifth gear, breathing hard, clearly ready to explode.

I tried to stop the moving train by telling him I wanted to go slower. I wanted to make the feeling last, but there was no stopping that bullet once it left the chamber. He was breathing hard, and I had stopped being involved in the process. I was no longer interested in this tired assault on my pussy.

Less than a minute later, he was tensing up and letting go. He collapsed on top of me, proud of himself for doing nothing special—aside from letting me down.

Why do all of the bad lays want to know if you enjoyed it? What are you supposed to say to that? Are you supposed to tell the truth? Are you supposed to say something harsh? "No, it was the worst dick I've ever had in my life."

Or do you return fire with a question of your own? "Did you not notice that I didn't make a sound and I stopped moving midway through the process?"

That day I was just a hole for him to put his stick into.

So when he asked the question all guys who are bad in bed ask, "Was it good?" I simply said, "Well, it was our first time together."

We tried it a couple more times after that, including one in the back of my SUV. I tried everything I could to make some magic that night.

I laid the seat back, got on top of him, and told him to suck my nipples until I said stop.

I loved it like nobody's business. This was our third time together, and I knew this time would be the game changer.

I was wet; I was ready; I was sure there was nothing he could do to ruin this. I'd positioned myself so that when I rode him I could feel the traction on my clit. All he had to do was last and stay where I put him. I had never worked so hard for an orgasm in all of my life. I realized I was in a race with a man to get mine before he got his—or it was going to be over.

I was humping like a woman on a mission, except it all backfired.

I inadvertently made him extra excited, forcing his hand—or his dick—to feel extra juiced up. Ah, hell, he was still going to cum before me.

After this final failed attempt at a mercy fuck, I gave up.

The next time he asked to "hook up," I just said no. He kept asking why I wouldn't, so he forced me to be honest with him. I told him it just wasn't good. Instead of him being embarrassed about it, he tried to talk me into doing it one more time, just to prove he could do it better.

I thought to myself, uh, hell naw, no thanks, I'm good.

You suck in bed. My sex number went up because of you, and I will no longer waste any of my good pussy juices on that unworthy dick.

No, we haven't done it again, just in case you were wondering.

Sometimes you just have to take the bull by the horns . . .
'Nuff said!

A Little Dick with My Dessert

There was this guy I was kind of digging on, Shane. We worked together and hung out a few times outside of work. I got the feeling he was feeling me too, but Shane wouldn't say it. He kind of showed it, by the way he hugged me.

Shane was the kind of man who liked to project a big, confident persona, but didn't have the balls to back it up. Truth be told, he was kind of a coward when it came to matters of the heart.

He was a little mysterious and made sure people saw him a certain way. I wanted to get inside of his head, see the real him, and get him to unravel a little.

Shane and I laughed a lot. We had fun hanging at festivals, going to intimate jazz concerts, and having drinks. I knew he liked me; I could feel it.

Now all I had to do was get him to act on it.

I'd been telling him how I can throw down in the kitchen, and I was about to use it to get what I wanted.

I decided I'd surprise him with some fried chicken. I told him I'd drop it off at his place. When I arrived, he had a surprise of his own: he'd baked me a pie.

Everything was pretty calm and low-key in the beginning.

I pulled out all of my tricks. I got hot and took off my top shirt, revealing my black and white cami with a nice

V-cut. The double D twins were rocking that night, but he only glanced.

I let Shane feed me caramel apple pie, but he still wouldn't touch me in a way that made me want to strip.

Everything was above board, even after I laughed and put my hand on his thigh.

He didn't move it, but he didn't encourage me to move it up either. I really thought I'd lost my touch.

Up until this very moment I'd never left a situation without getting what I wanted, which was usually having the object of my affection slowly or viciously tearing off my clothes, opening my legs, and making me writhe with pleasure.

So far, this was a big fat dud, so I was about to find something else to do with my time. I told him I was about to go. He asked if I was sure.

Of course I was sure; this was some boring mess. I was going home to have more action with my vibrator—I was wet. Now I was forced to take care of things myself. Shane walked me to the door, told me how great the chicken looked, and how he couldn't wait to try it.

Yeah, yeah, yeah, I thought, let me get the hell out of here.

He was standing at the door giving me this long ass goodbye.

I don't know what happened. Maybe my eyes glazed over from being so bored. Maybe I knew he wanted me and was too chicken to do anything about it. Or maybe it was the fact that I never left a hunt without my prey.

Whatever it was it made me pin my body against his body as he tried to hug me goodbye. He kind of fell against the door, and before he could regain his footing I was kissing him. He was shocked. He caught on quickly to what was happening—at least, that's what his dick was telling me. I felt it harden inside of his jeans against my leg. He was trying to get the upper hand, but it was too late for that: I was in control now, and I didn't plan on letting it go. My body was in overdrive. He undid my pants, slipped his fingers inside of my thong, and felt just how much I wanted him.

I moaned inside of his mouth as my tongue continued to attack him.

I was furious in my actions; he needed to know he could've had all of me, had he not wasted so much time.

All was not lost, I thought, as he parted my thighs, trying his best to make me rain on his fingers. I felt like he was going to get the upper hand.

I changed tactics. I was undoing his pants as I sucked his lower lip.

I asked him if he wanted me. He said yes, and seconds later I was on my knees, swiftly freeing him from his boxer briefs.

I'm pretty sure Shane didn't know what happened, but I knew what was about to happen. I devoured him. His dick disappeared inside of my mouth before he knew what was going on.

He wanted to go to the couch, upstairs, anywhere to take advantage of what was going on at the back door in his kitchen.

His arms dropped to his sides.

I heard him say he didn't know I could do that with my mouth; that just fueled my hunger. I was slow and deliberate, dragging my tongue over every morsel. My mouth was watering just listening to the sounds of pleasure.

He grabbed my head with both hands, trying to make me go at his rhythm. His time for calling the shots was over for the evening.

I stopped, removed his hands, and told him to relax and let me take care of him. I promised him he would love it.

I drank him in, picking up my speed. My tongue was like a tornado on him.

He was trying to touch any part of my body he could reach. He was close, I could feel it. My head was bobbing rhythmically, and I couldn't help but moan a little. I couldn't wait to see what he tasted like. Just as I thought it, I felt him gush inside of my mouth.

Hmmm, not bad, I thought.

He helped me up off of my knees and simply said, "Wow."

Yeah, I know, I thought.

He wanted a round two, but I was ready to go. I had to work too hard to get this. It was his turn to work to get it back.

If he wanted me, he had better come after me. Tonight was just the beginning of our game.

Who doesn't like long walks in the park, holding hands with that special someone?

While I may not admit it, I do enjoy those moments of solitude, especially at night, when you think no one is watching.

That's when a walk in the park becomes something more.

A Walk in the Park or Something Like That

I was at the gas station filling up my car when I felt someone's eyes on me.

I turned to the side to see where the stare was coming from. It was some guy across the parking lot filling up his car. He smiled. I, of course, smiled right back. I was wearing some revealing cut-off jean shorts with an extra rip up the right side—so ripped you could see the lining of the pocket.

I made a show of bending so he could see what I was working with, and believe me, there was plenty of sexy back there.

He finished first, so he drove up next to me and introduced himself. His name was Lane.

I gave him my sly smile, the one where I go for innocent with a little bit of harlot.

I shifted my weight to poke my booty out just a little; can't show your whole hand up front. I told him my name; of course he said it was nice to meet me. What else would you say to someone you're trying to pick up at a gas station?

He was trying to figure out what type of woman I was. Was I going to play his game or shoot him down?

I was assessing him as well. He had a smooth chocolate complexion.

He was wearing glasses, his lips were thick, and he was semicute. I'd play his game, but he was on a timer. He asked if I had a man. I said no, and from there he gave me his number. He presumed I wanted it. I liked the confidence, but I knew I wasn't going to call him. I think he had the same feeling, so he asked me for my number, and I gave it to him.

He called that night. We met for lunch the next day, and that bought him one more try for something.

That "something" was the next night, when he called to see what I was doing. He wanted to come over and spend some time with me.

I didn't want him to know where I lived, so I agreed to meet him at the park in my subdivision. I walked down to meet him and we chatted for a moment, but let's be real— neither one of us had that much to say.

He pulled me close to him and started kissing me. His arms were stronger than I imagined. He made me want to be there.

He ran one of his hands down my back, stopped at my ass, and grabbed.

He kissed me deeper and harder. Ohh, he was making me hot and wet.

This virtual stranger removed his hand from my behind and moved both hands up my back, and around to my breasts.

I didn't wear a bra that night, and I was glad I didn't. He didn't have to work at removing it. I could tell he was pleasantly surprised, so much so that he broke away from my lips and put his mouth on my naked nips.

I didn't complain. I let him know I liked it with a nice little moan as my head fell back. We were near a slide, and we were about to defile it.

He sat me on the slide, got on his knees, and unbuttoned my shorts. I lifted myself just enough to let him slide them down.

He put his middle finger inside of my vagina to test the waters, and there was a warm flood. I heard him say "mmm," as if he was about to taste some very sweet nectar—and boy, was he ever.

He didn't take off my panties; he just moved them to the side. Then I felt his tongue.

It was silky, broad, and everything I thought about. Those thick lips were true; he had some skills.

I leaned back on the slide and let him handle his business.

I was feeling it. I put my hands under my shirt and caressed my own tits.

I tried to remember we were in a park in a residential area and there was no room for wailing like a banshee.

That's when I noticed his tongue was gone, replaced by two fingers deep inside of me, finishing the job his tongue began.

He let his thumb rub over my clit gently, so light it sent shivers through my body.

I was on the verge of a great explosion, one that needed to stay under control.

I put one leg over his shoulder to give my orgasm room to release, and ohhh it was so good, made more powerful by the fact that I had to stifle it. The intensity of my orgasm powered through my body, making me shake.

I thanked him by undoing his pants and taking his hard dick into my mouth.

I wanted him to walk away weak. I took him deep in my throat and let it linger. He was feeling good, and I knew it. He gripped my shoulders. I slowly pulled my mouth back, keeping a firm grip on his dick.

I let my tongue tickle the underside of his penis. I didn't just want him—I wanted power over him.

I went to work, throwing my sucking into overdrive. He grabbed my hair. He wanted to guide my head, but I knew what I was doing, and I didn't need his help.

I put my hand up; he got the point.

His dick was wet with my excitement. I was grunting and groaning with every stroke. His breathing was shallow and quicker; he was about to blow.

I went faster, and then I felt the warm prize I was going for—yeah, I swallow.

It was a good night, one that wasn't repeated.

I didn't answer any more of his calls, not because I thought he was a bad guy, but I knew from day one he wasn't someone I was interested in getting to know. I just wanted to have a little summertime fun.

"It hurts so good." There was a time when I didn't know what that meant.

There was a time when I only wanted to be spanked, and maybe have my hair pulled. But there's more than that.

A little tweak, a little twist, and a little pinch—but oh yes, there is so much more.

The S & M Experiment

I wasn't sure what was going to happen. I was lying there exposed.

I was the one who said I wanted to try something new. We had an amateur bondage set that only required us to connect four pieces and anchor it under the mattress, no bedposts required. There was a whip and tickler, plus a vibrator with five speeds. I'd seen the videos of women being tied up, whipped, and taken by their dominators. It was kind of primitive, but that's what made it so hot. These women would beg for the chance to cum. Tonight I was about to see what it was all about.

Sure, I'd been spanked while bent over, which always made me bounce my booty a little more. I'd done some things with nipple clamps. The painful pinch forced all of the sensations to gather in one place, making it so sensitive you had no choice but to shudder uncontrollably when you hit the top. It was the pleasure of the pain. I'd wanted to try it for a while, but I was a little apprehensive about going there.

This night, I'd found the courage to give up complete control of my body. Tonight I was about to get what I asked for.

I got the feeling he was going to enjoy this more than he let on. I was the experimental one when it came to our sex life. While he was always willing to go above and beyond when it came to pleasing me, I was surprised when he said yes to my latest request, because I knew I was pushing our boundaries.

Tonight he was my commander; I was to submit to his will. This night we were strangers: no names, no history.

I was on my back; my legs were spread and cuffed. My arms saw the same fate. He left me there alone in his room, barely able to move. I was anticipating what was about to happen.

I was about to get my first taste of what it felt like to be bound and fucked. This was going to be the night I found out what it meant to not be in charge of my own orgasms.

My heart was already pounding and he hadn't even touched me.

My elation was seeping from inside of me as I waited for him to return to the room.

When he walked back in, he grinned in a way that let me know he was going to take full advantage of this opportunity to guide my every feeling. I immediately felt anxious and wanted to somehow free myself because part of me wondered if I could yield completely to him. I was smiling because I was nervous. He was smirking because the queen of control was now under his command.

The wait was over. It was time to start our little private party. I wondered what he had in store for me. I kept moving my fingers and feet as if I could actually do something to influence my own fate.

He started slowly. I think it was because he was still feeling his way through this process. All that did was make me more antsy.

Then I felt something: the light touch of the feather tickler being swept up my leg to my thigh, up my midsection to my left breast, and then over to my right breast. I inhaled deeply as the fun began. He brushed the feathers back down my body, paying special attention to my inner thighs. We were silent as the game began. He switched the tickler with the cat-o'-nine-tails whip and circled the thin leather straps around my midsection slowly before slapping me lightly with it. It felt strange at first because I couldn't believe we were doing this, but he was fulfilling my fantasy.

I was about to smile when he hit me across the breasts. It didn't hurt, but it did shock me a little. It seemed my fantasy-filler was getting into his part. I felt my hips rise up a little bit. I tried to bend my legs as if I could capture the feeling, but I was quickly reminded of my present situation. I heard the metal *cling* as the cuffs jerked my feet back into place. I felt all of the wetness overflowing from my pussy. I wondered if he knew how much he was turning me on. It was more than being tied to his bed with the threat of a tickler and whip—it was the fact that he said yes to my desire, and he was having fun with it.

I wanted to reach for him to thank him, but my efforts were stopped by the padded bracelets on my wrists.

He brushed the tickler against my pussy, and it made me want to open my legs even more for him. When he turned the whip back to me, I actually found myself wanting him to use it on me, to give me the attention my body was yearning for, even if it would result in my skin stinging a little. He got me again. I knew he was taking it easy on me. I knew he didn't want to hurt me, not even accidentally, not even if there was a possibility I would like it . . . and I liked it. (I'm sure he could tell by how easy it was to pull my nipples because they were so erect.)

He hovered over me, looking at me as if he was trying to figure out what he was going to do to me next.

I finally told him how wet I was. He said he already knew; he'd already felt the essence. He probably singed his hands a little from the heat radiating from down there.

Then I felt nothing. He'd stopped. That's when I realized I had closed my eyes. I heard rustling. He was going for the vibrator on the nightstand. My heart was beating faster. I wasn't watching him anymore. Part of me wanted to be surprised by what was coming next, and there was a part of me that was trying to relax and enjoy the ride.

I heard the familiar buzz of my favorite toy. I felt the vibrations along the inside of my thigh. It was just close enough to the tip of my release valve, but he wouldn't give me the direct pressure I so desperately wanted. He let that vibrator seduce every other inch of space between my legs. He put it inside of me, and he circled it around my plump pussy lips. He brushed it over my clit, repeatedly bringing me to the brink of orgasm, but he refused to allow me to finish. Sadly, I loved it. It made me even more eager for his touch. With my wrists and ankles restrained, I couldn't even manipulate the vibrator or his hands to the one spot where all of my happiness was stored.

I couldn't wait anymore. I didn't want to wait anymore. I decided to let my very sexy captor know where to put it. I told him to leave it on my sex button. I was sure he was going to do just what I asked of him, so I was shocked when he stopped and asked me who was in charge. I quickly answered, "You are, daddy."

He allowed the toy to touch me again as he told me he "had this" . . . he was in charge. I knew I was pressing my luck when I told him I wanted to cum with a little too much authority in my voice. I think I thought if I was my normal assertive self during this tryst he'd just want me to be pleased and do it. Tonight that was not the case. My lover had quickly adapted to his role as master over his vixen. He told me I could cum when he let me. All that did was make my desire for him and my elusive waterfall grow. I tried once again to move my body closer to him or anything that would put out the fire inside of me. The flood in my pussy was like gasoline spilling out, further igniting the flame. "Can I please cum?" I asked him. Actually, I was now begging. The more I pleaded, the more I struggled, and the more he held me at bay. I now understood how the women in the videos ended up begging. I was taken to a point of release, but wasn't allowed to turn the faucet on. I teetered on the edge of pure pleasure and torture, and I was now desperate for relief.

I tried to bring my thighs together in hopes of sneaking a little extra pressure, but those damn ankle cuffs kept snatching me back in place. He kept asking me if I wanted to cum. "Yes please, please daddy can I cum?" I could feel my insides trembling. If I could only get to the vibrator, his fingers—anything—to help relieve the torment.

He was watching me, seemingly enjoying every second of this body takeover.

He told me to beg for it; it was what he wanted to hear.

I pleaded for him to let me have it as I wiggled any free body part as close to him as I could. He had this look of enjoyment on his face, as if he too were surprised at how much he liked hearing this control freak of a woman beg at his whim.

He asked me if I wanted it. I made sure this time I was polite when I answered, "Yes, please." I was on the brink. I didn't need much provocation, just him to put pressure in the right place.

I asked him again if I could please, please cum. I heard a chuckle in his voice when he said, "Yes, you can," as he unleashed the vibrations on my spot.

The delayed gratification of my orgasm under restriction made me pull and yank on the ties that bound me. I felt relief, but I was still thirsty because I had yet to feel the power of his dick inside of me.

I didn't know when I'd get it. He had completely taken on the role of controller.

My sexy knight paused for a moment and looked down at me before straddling my face.

He wasn't going to give me the dick just yet, but at least I was going to be allowed to taste him.

I was able to raise my head off the bed to meet all of that thickness with my mouth. I wrapped my tongue around him in an attempt to draw him in deep. He knew how to drag out the sexy torture. He knew I wanted nothing more than to have him inside of me, but he also knew I couldn't resist guzzling him, feeling his power down my throat. As strong as he was, he still managed to show restraint as I tried to keep up with his rhythm. He pulled out of my mouth, and yet again I was left wanting more of him. I asked him if I could touch him.

I pulled my head up again to kiss him. Our lips met briefly before he removed himself from my reach. I still couldn't move. I still couldn't get to him. I still couldn't wrap my arms and legs around his body. There was no way for me to get him to enter me to stop the dripping. I simply said, "Please."

"Please what?" he wanted to know. I told him I wanted him inside of me, but I wasn't specific enough for him. He asked what I wanted inside of me.

"Your dick," I told him. I was thinking, it's my dick, I want my dick, but I was afraid to say it aloud out of fear he would make me wait longer. He was finally positioning himself between my legs. My pussy was heating up more from the anticipation. He was so hard, and had so much strength. I tried to raise my hips to meet him. He towered over me, and his dick danced around my pussy. I knew I was drenching him even though he wasn't inside of me—that's how much I wanted him at that moment.

"Can I please have it, daddy?" I kept asking. I could tell he was enjoying this, maybe a little too much. The game of keep away continued. He put it right there at the entrance, but he was finally ready.

He had to let my legs loose to get inside of me. Just as I thought, great, he's letting me go, he tells me, "Just the legs." At that point, I was willing to take what I could get. He kept my legs apart as he plunged into me.

I tried to bring his face to me, but again I was reminded that how and when I moved wasn't up to me. I was his love slave for the night. I swear I heard him chuckle at yet another failed attempt to move toward him. He stayed inside of me as he brought my legs together, trapping the good feelings, causing the pressure to build up between my closed thighs. He moved my legs to the right side as he worked meticulously on making my body succumb to his will.

He let my legs rest on his shoulder, but he didn't stop the drilling. The harder I tried to meet his thrusts without the use of my arms, the closer I came to cumming.

He grabbed my nipples and twisted them without applying any pressure. There was something so sexy about how he managed to pull without pain. His touch was so gentle, yet it sent shockwaves through all of me. I was on the brink; the explosion was inevitable. I tried to kiss him again, but he was just out of reach. I didn't want to play this game anymore. I was ready to climb the walls, if only my hands were free.

My sexy lover was deep inside of me as if he was driving the orgasm out of me. At this rate he wasn't going to have to wait too much longer. I was crying for him as the dam burst, squirting my appreciation all over him. All I could do was thank him for allowing me such an aggressive release.

He kissed me, then let me know he was going to release me. First he undid the left wrist. I immediately put my free arm around him. I almost didn't care the other arm was still in a bind. I just needed to touch his face, his body, bring him closer to me, as if that would somehow melt him inside of me.

He released my second hand. I wanted so much more of him. Keeping me in captivity like that made me damn near insatiable. If I could've climbed him at that moment I would have. Instead, I wrapped my legs tighter around him. I grabbed his face and damn near forced his mouth to mine. I felt like I needed to take back a little bit of control, but that didn't last. The "stranger" taking me to extreme heights of excitement wasn't having any of that. Honestly, at this point, I didn't care. He'd proven that being the master in charge was highly beneficial to the pleasure of my pussy.

Even though we were strangers for the night, our bodies didn't forget who we were to each other.

We were long time distant lovers. There was no amount of role-play that could disguise our chemistry. Our bodies spoke to each other when we were too overcome with lust to use words.

He demanded that I grab it. He wanted me to use my pussy as a steel trap. I was more than happy to do anything he told me to do.

He turned up the heat on his stroke, harder and faster. I was absorbing everything he had to offer. I may not have been tied down anymore, but I was still under his command. I dared not make a move without his approval. I didn't know where the whip was—not that he needed one, since he used his hand to slap my cheeks again and again, filling me to the brim with want until I popped like balloon.

More, more, I thought to myself.

I kept calling myself his cum whore. I couldn't stop; I was lost in emotion. I had been bound, tickled in every sensitive area, whipped, and forced to teeter on the edge of orgasm repeatedly.

I could only imagine what he was feeling as he told me it was okay, reminding me that this was how it was supposed to be.

This is what magic was supposed to feel like between two people who were friends and lovers, even though we were "strangers" for this night. My "mystery man" wasn't through with me yet.

He brought me to the edge of the bed. He had an ankle in each hand as he stood over me at attention. I was always impressed with his stamina. He plunged back into my throbbing but still starving hole like a deep-sea diver.

He was making me feel out of control, making me once again moan out another show of appreciation for my master of the evening. He lay down next to me as I tried to catch my breath and compose myself.

He was smiling, clearly satisfied with his own performance.

As I looked over at him, I wanted more. I couldn't believe my insides were still calling out for him, as tired as I was.

Never one to disappoint, he was ready to mount me again, but the entryway had closed, swollen shut from over-indulgence. All we could do was laugh and rest up for the next time. Maybe next time he'd let me tie him down.

A night of fantasies with friends and strangers.

It was a time to let go of your inhibitions and let your body guide you to the next thrill and release.

The Other Side: Part 2

What do you do after you've had the most intense orgasm in your sexual life? You don't just lie there, that's for sure. You return the favor.

I didn't know what I was doing. I wasn't sure if I was as good of a pleasure giver for these women as I was a pleasure seeker, but I was definitely going to do my very best and hope to taste the juices of satisfaction.

I could see the fellas. They looked as if they were watching a live flick, and they had front row seats.

There was a mix of glee and eagerness etched across their faces.

One of them said, "Your turn." They knew they were in for a rare treat. They were lucky; they were viewers of a very sensuous show.

Yes, it was my turn to perform, and I needed to earn a standing ovation.

I whispered to the girls that I didn't know what I was doing. They told me not to worry about it, and just take my time.

I sat up in the bed and smiled. I took a shot of vodka and a hit from the blunt being passed.

I was nervous but excited and unafraid. My first taste would be the girl who brought her own collar and chain. There was something so alluring about her; she didn't have a model body, but she was secure in her sexiness. I felt like when she looked me in the eyes, we connected, and I knew she would guide me. Now, it was show time.

I straddled her body and brushed my lips across hers. They were softer than mine; however, I didn't linger too long—this isn't what the men wanted to see.

They wanted to see my body move over hers, they wanted to see my back arch, they wanted to see my mouth on her nipples—so that's where I placed them. I let them see my tongue touch them before letting my lips wrap them up. I listened for a sign she was enjoying this at least a little bit. I heard it in her sigh. Her breathing was heavy, but so was mine.

Was I getting that turned on from sucking the breasts of a woman? I had to admit, it did get me going to be able to feed someone's desires in that way, but it wasn't just me doing what I was doing. The taller, hourglass-built girl had inserted two fingers inside of me. I was subconsciously rotating my hips around them.

She used that influence to guide me down my girl's body to her pussy.

One of them told me to lick it. I was scared of what it would taste like; up to that point I had only tasted myself. Would she taste as good as I did?

Seconds later I knew: she was sweet. My instincts took over from there. I knew how I liked it, and I was about to see if she liked it the same way. I sucked her clit as if I was drinking from a straw. I was still riding her friend's fingers. It encouraged me to do everything to my fullest ability.

I alternated between sucking and tickling with my tongue. I wanted more; I wanted to go deeper. I moved my mouth farther down south to taste everything.

The other girl removed her fingers from inside of me and moved up to kiss her friend on the mouth while I continued to push my tongue deeper inside of her. She moved her hips up to meet my mouth; she was enjoying it way more than

I thought she would. It made me work harder to pull the pleasure from her.

I went back to her clit and let the roughness of my tongue massage her there. I knew she was about to cum; she was moving in time with me. I heard her moan, I felt her tensing up, and then she announced she was cumming. I smiled, impressed with myself.

The fellas could no longer take it. My man was behind me. He pulled me up, pulled my head back, and kissed the other woman's juices from my mouth. It was so sexy; I wanted to feel him inside of me immediately.

He didn't even turn me around, he just bent me over in front of her and entered me from behind.

I knew he was turned on; he was almost growling as he slammed himself against me. It was one of those hurt-so-good feelings.

There was no way I could be quiet on this one. I didn't mind my manners and try to be respectful of others.

The two other fellas were with their ladies by now.

The one I hadn't pleased yet was next to me on her back. I don't know what came over me, but she was close enough for me to reach her, so I kissed her as her man fucked her. This made my man spank me, hard, the way I liked it. It made me scream and laugh a little at the same time.

He pulled me up without coming out of me and asked me if I was happy. I said yes as he pushed me back down. I knew he was about to let go, and I wanted to meet him there. I reached between my legs and helped myself speed up my process.

The sound of everyone's enjoyment was intoxicating—it was like being drunk in a club and the music becomes a hollow backdrop in your ear. That's what it was like as I came hard again, but I didn't want to stop. The night was young, we had hours to go, and there were four people I still hadn't sampled.

Sometimes you find yourself in a situation where you have lost all self-control.

You know what you're doing is wrong, but you can't help it because part of you is drunk with the power that you have over this person. The other part of you is too weakened by the power he has over you to put up the good fight, and that makes what you're doing 100 times hotter.

Oops!

I'm not sure how it happened, but it shouldn't have happened.

One minute we were arguing, the next minute I was pulling my panties up in the parking lot of a park, after dark.

That night still seems so unreal to me. I didn't want to do it. I didn't even want it, or so I thought.

We went for a ride after having one of our famous arguments that seemed to only serve as foreplay.

My ex and I were at his mother's house. I had stopped by to say hello to her.

Even though her son, Josh, and I weren't together anymore, she and I were still close. I didn't expect to see him—I wasn't sure if I wanted to see him—but there he was, right in front of me. It was always a little awkward when we stood under the same roof or shared the same space; you could feel the electricity.

It's not something I wanted to feel, needed to feel, or could afford to feel. Josh knew it was there, and he capitalized on it.

We were never really cordial to each other. A little hostility always lingered between us, which served as a powerful magnet no matter what I did to escape it.

We faked our hellos, and I felt the charge as he smacked me on my ass, as he so often did.

You see, Josh had a terrible time keeping his hands to himself when he was near me. A part of me liked it, and liked it a lot.

The other part of me hated myself for even having feelings for someone who didn't deserve my attention—but here I was, standing next to him with a tingle down there.

I saw something different in him for a few moments: it was something I hadn't seen or felt in years.

For a little while, I remembered why I used to love him. Our conversations were always easy, and we had fun. The fun we had always led to some really good times between the sheets, in the back seat of a car, or in the shower.

But those days were over, even if my nipples were getting hard every time he "accidentally" brushed up against my breasts.

We played our game masterfully that night. I pretended to be annoyed, and he pretended to be disgusted by my attitude as he pulled my hair when he walked past me.

He knew what tickled my sweet spot, and pulling my hair was one of those things.

My wild, natural hair was like an aphrodisiac to him, and every time he grabbed a handful it was a direct line to my pussy.

Before that night, whenever he touched my booty, grabbed my breasts, or tried to put his hands on my vagina, I'd always been able to resist, to repel his advances. But that day, he touched my hair.

He went for the jugular. When he pulled, my head went back and I wanted to kiss him. However, I didn't tell him that; I would never admit to having any feelings toward him—but again, here we were.

He asked me to ride to the store with him. I hesitated, but eventually agreed.

Why did I do that, why did I say yes?

We rode around for a little while. You could feel the heat; you could sense what was going to happen.

It was so strong—you could smell the thought of sex on us. We were quiet until he asked me if I wanted him.

Of course I said no. There was no way I was admitting to wanting him, even if my body was gravitating toward his.

It was dark. I told him we should head back to his mom's house. He agreed, but didn't turn around.

Instead, we ended up in an empty park parking lot. No good could come of this.

He told me to get out of the car. I refused. I really didn't want to go down that path with him.

He opened my door and demanded I get out. I still wouldn't.

He reached in, grabbed a handful of hair, and started kissing me. I was overwhelmed by the force of his tongue. I got out of the car as he commanded. He grabbed me and pulled me into him and kissed me again, but this time was different. It was as if he was now trying to fight his own feelings.

He abruptly pulled away, but decided to punish my body. He started trying to take my pants down. I tried to keep him from succeeding, but it only served as what used to be our normal foreplay. It made me instinctively push my body toward him as I simultaneously tried to pull away. He had his hands up my shirt, manipulating my nipples. Oh my, what a feeling. The feelings were all rushing back to me, and they were good. I still kept fighting it, but somehow my pants were around my ankles now. I heard him undo his pants. It was going to happen.

He didn't remove my thong; he simply moved it over. He kissed my neck, then pushed me over the hood of his car.

He put his dick inside of me, and we both let out this sigh—it was like we hadn't missed a beat, but we missed how we made each other feel. He whispered in my ear that I felt so good, so wet, he missed me—he missed this.

I did too for that moment, but I couldn't tell him that; it was only for the moment.

He used those minutes to make himself at home inside of me, reminding me of what it was we used to share.

He used his time to make me holler.

It was cold outside, but my insides were hot. The breeze did little to cool us down.

We were like two dogs. He'd mounted me, all right; a water hose couldn't have separated us.

He kept asking me if I missed him. It made me want him more, for the moment.

Hearing him tell me he wanted me made me let him have his way with me. And just like that, it was over, and we were silent.

He asked me if I was okay. What was I going to say? I got back in the car and said nothing for a while.

He told me how good it still was. He wanted to know if I felt the same way. Of course I did, but I couldn't say it aloud—I didn't want any of it back. It was a blip in time; it was an oops that would never happen again . . . well, until the next time it happened . . . Oops!

When the person you love doesn't show up for you, there is always someone else waiting to fill the void. If you don't want someone else loving your love, step up!

Filling the Void

My accent guy was up for all kinds of forbidden fun.

One day in particular, I was in need of a new man to fill the void left by my man, who had once again broken our plans.

I called my island man because I was in need of some attention.

I was straight up with him, letting him know what was about to happen and why I was calling him. About 30 seconds into the conversation, he told me he'd meet me at my hotel room, the one my man reserved for our special evening together.

I was barely dressed in a shirt and thong when my islander arrived.

I felt bad about what I was about to do until he pulled me in and hugged me. He made me feel like he missed me, like he wanted me. I knew he dropped what he was doing to come see me, something my man still hadn't mastered. This made me want my islander even more. I just started taking his clothes off. As I kissed him, I got hungrier and hungrier; he was my appetizer, main course, and dessert. He didn't know what hit him. He finally caught up with me fast, and kicked off his shoes while I undid his pants. I dropped to my knees, pulled them down for him, and pulled his dick out of his boxer briefs without even removing them. I couldn't wait; I was salivating all over his piece. I was angry, and someone or something had to pay—it just so happened to be his dick.

One thing about my island man: he wasn't going to let me be in control for long. He was an alpha male. He pulled me back by my hair, knowing how much taking control turned me on. He sat me on the couch in the room, my cue to spread my legs. I tore off my shirt, exposing my bare breasts. I had taken off my bra long before he got there.

We were a little awkward. We couldn't find our rhythm, and it was frustrating me because I really wanted to cum.

I leaned into his mouth as I grabbed a breast in each hand and pinched my own nipples. I rotated my hips on him, trying to get some juice. It just wasn't working.

I got up to switch positions, thinking if he were on the bottom, we would get some traction.

It worked for a second. I was wet again, feeling wild; I wanted him, yet our dance was clumsy.

I was about to give up, but he suggested we use the bed. Instead of getting up, I let myself slide to the floor to pout, naked.

Maybe something about seeing me vulnerable was a major turn on, because the next thing I knew he was turning me on my knees in front of the couch. He pulled my hips toward him and rammed himself inside of me. Maybe he was frustrated too. He had my shoulders. I felt like I didn't have a choice but to take it. We'd found our rhythm.

He spanked me while asking if this was how I wanted it.

I could only say yes, because it was what I wanted— more than he knew. He tried one more time to get to the bed, but I just ended up on my hands and knees, the perfect position for domination. He commanded me to just stay there in that accent. I just said, "Okay."

He spread my legs and pushed my head toward the floor. I felt like I was his blow-up doll; I felt like he was punishing me for making him the standby guy.

My island man was relentless. I could feel the carpet burns forming on my knees, but I didn't care.

There was a man banging me from behind in a room my boyfriend paid for. We were now in a full-fledged frenzy on that floor.

His long dick always hit the spot. It was such a nice feeling: the tingling, the passionate pain, the lack of control I had when I was with him. It was a recipe for eruption.

Ahhh, I heard myself getting louder, a sign of bliss. I wanted to feel a double-dose of ecstasy, so I reached between my legs to help speed up my orgasm.

He was thrusting, and I was stroking my clit. Ohh, it was so great, so great.

My release was thunderous. I could feel my walls holding onto his beautiful dick. There was no rest for me; he wanted to get his too. He liked it when I rode him, so he flipped to his back on the floor. Who needed a bed, anyway?

My thick, wet, still-pulsating pussy took over his dick. I leaned back to rock him into submission. I knew how he liked it; I knew how he wanted it. He wanted me to lean back as far as I could so he could see the top of my breasts. He liked how the nipples danced as I rolled back and forth on all of that manliness.

I could hear him say he was close. I knew what I needed to do, because all this bouncing was making me tired—a girl could only stay leaned back for so long.

I came forward, sitting straight so I could bounce on the full length of him. Sitting up on it was making me want to have another—a delightful side effect of riding a stallion of sorts. Now we were both breathing hard. He was closer to the edge than I was; now I had some catching up to do.

I leaned in close to him so I could get my clit the much-needed attention to reach peak performance. I didn't have to worry about if he was going to get his because I was so juicy. I was pouring all over him. By the time he said he was cumming, I was cumming again too. It was so fierce, it caused me to speed up my reps—it was a rapid-fire bounce.

I collapsed right on top of him. He told me he'd missed me. I missed him too; he was my go-to guy when I was in town.

I was no longer angry with my man for standing me up.

When my man did finally arrive, I would be nice and warmed up for him. Until then, I let my island man caress my body while he was still inside of me, reenergizing himself for round two.

When a man wants you, I mean *really* wants you, there isn't anything he won't do to have you.

He will chase. He will find any excuse to get you alone, to talk to you, to breathe your scent, to feel you, to take you—no matter what the cost.

Don't Speak

He was knocking at my door, even though I told him he should go home to his wife.

He called me about 15 minutes ago. I didn't realize he was so close.

I guess part of me really wanted him to show up; otherwise, I wouldn't have given him my address.

Let me explain that one . . . I could tell he had been drinking when he called. He asked if he could come over; of course I said no. It had been some time since we'd been together. I wasn't supposed to be with him. He had a wife—it didn't matter that he wasn't happy with her. She was still very real.

It didn't matter that he made me climb the walls, literally. It all had to stop.

So when he called me to say he wanted to come over, my mind said yes but I forced my mouth to say no.

I gave him my address because he said it was the only way he would go home. He promised he would go home—only he didn't go home.

There was a knock on my door. I opened it, and without warning, his lips were covering mine. He sucked in my air; I didn't mind not breathing for those few seconds.

I gasped and tried to tell him to go home, but all I could manage was a deep, intoxicating breath.

He pushed me up against the wall and kissed me hard. I could taste the liquor on his tongue; it kind of turned me on.

He was willing to risk a lot to see me because he wanted to be inside of me again.

He closed the door with his foot but he never took his eyes off of me. I felt like he could see my heart pounding and my soul joining his.

He put my arms above my head and used those beautiful lips to kiss my neck. When I lightly resisted, he pushed me back into the wall, grabbed my right nipple hard, and twisted it through my tank top.

It made me twist with anticipation—my pussy was wet. I lunged my waist toward him, but I couldn't get any closer to him since my arms were still pinned to the wall. He whispered how much he wanted me, then put his free hand down my shorts. I didn't have any underwear on, by the way, so he ran into a liquid fun-fest. I spread my legs, inviting his fingers to come into me as far as he could manage. I put one leg around his waist to bring him closer to me.

He reached down and exposed my breasts. It was as if they were calling his name, the way he sucked them first, then bit them.

It was the most pleasurable pain I'd felt in quite some time. I didn't have a lot of words, and neither did he.

He stopped, looked at me, and then reached for the door, as if he was silently asking if I wanted him to leave. I didn't want him to go, but I tried to be strong and responsible. I broke what seemed to be our unspoken vow of silence by telling him I thought it would be a good idea. He asked if I was sure. I said no—he bit my breast as a sign of his pleasure. I didn't want to be marked; we were both "taken."

Through my labored breathing I managed to tell him to go to my room.

I grabbed him by his hand and pulled him behind me. Once that door was closed I ripped off my clothes.

I was naked before he was. He showed his appreciation by opening my lower lips with his tongue.

He licked me, swirling his tongue around my clit. I took in a deep breath—my body wanted to cum. It had been waiting for him to come back. I spread my legs so I could take in every single lick and tingle. I wanted to yell, but the screams kept getting caught in my throat. It was just so good. What I felt for him was so strong; maybe it was because I wasn't supposed to be feeling the love, lust, and intense attraction to this man.

I grabbed his head. His hair was so soft, which added to my already heightened state of arousal. I was so close to the edge, and he knew it.

He came up for air, and I wanted to taste myself on him. I licked his lips as I kissed him. I felt so wanted, so out of control, so ravaged.

He stood up, leaving me wanting again, but not for long.

The man who inhaled my soul when he walked into the door was now taking off his pants, his shirt, and his boxer briefs.

I lay there in awe of his lean, toned body.

I wanted him in a way I hadn't wanted anyone else in a while. I felt so close to him. I wanted to rush through it, but he wanted to take his time.

He knew he wasn't supposed to be with me. We'd talked about it, but now here he was, about to enter me again.

This time we weren't standing against a wall, trying to maintain balance—he was lying me down, kissing every part of my body, as if I were a precious gem.

He couldn't get enough of me, and I couldn't get enough of him. Finally, he let himself into me.

Again, I was breathless and speechless. It was so easy the way he penetrated me, as if he was meant to be there: so smooth, so soft, and so rough at the same time.

I whispered, "Thank you, thank you for making every inch of my body feel good, for making me feel like I was soaring, for sucking my nipples and making them thick and pointed." He blew them dry as his dick stroked in and out of me. My moans were louder and louder.

My legs were climbing his body. I wanted him deeper; I was willing to bend in any direction to allow myself to take in all of his body with my vagina.

The pressure was building. He kept asking if I was enjoying it. "Yes, yes baby."

I didn't mean to call him baby—it just slipped out, and I didn't try to take it back. He liked it, and kissed me long and hard as my reward.

I liked this side of him; he was always so sweet and gentle whenever he interacted with me.

It was something I loved about him. This in-control man who was making me writhe in pure pleasure made me leak with joy.

He was about to accomplish what he came here to do, and that was to make me have a great orgasm.

He was about to have one too, but not before me. "Harder," I demanded, and he complied immediately.

My body responded just as quickly; my hips met every forceful thrust. More; more; I wanted more.

He kept it coming. I didn't realize I was holding my breath until I released it, and I was hit by a wave of shock and gratification. "Oh my goodness," was all I could get out before my body went limp. I felt him collapse on top of me after his release.

I wanted him to stay, but I knew he couldn't. I knew it wouldn't be right, but I said it aloud anyway. I knew the response would bring disappointment, but I wanted him to know I wanted him to stay. I had him for the next few moments before he kissed me at the door, the way he came in. Then he was gone.

There are times when you get wrapped up in great—no, phenomenal—sex, and you're repeatedly blinded to that man's shortcomings. His rudeness and lies take a back seat to good sense.

But once you come to your senses, it's over for that person, PERIOD!

Just Like That

Just like that, I was sucked back into his web, after I had finally managed to get him out of my system. I could talk to him without getting wet and wanting to crawl through the phone so he could touch and feast on every suckable part of my body.

But one phone call from him seemed to have changed all of that. It was a pleasant surprise to hear his voice on the other end of my phone tonight.

He told me he was at the grocery store doing some shopping and I crossed his mind.

We hadn't talked for a while, and I was okay with that. There was a time when he'd turned my life upside down because I was so hooked on his dick.

It was so good, so potent, and so reliable; I couldn't seem to get enough.

From the first time he sat me down under a tree one mild summer day, lifted my dress to my waist, and buried his head between my legs, he was the magic man in my life. Michael was an amazing lover. He had the ability to push my buttons with his fingers, tongue, and his very well endowed dick. He was like my drug. I couldn't kick the habit—even when he lied to me, kept me hanging on with false hope, and always chose another over me. We would argue, but it was like the sex—it just got better with every disagreement. I hated and loved him at the same time.

There were days when we would meet up for "lunch" or "breakfast," but the only things on the menu were my pussy and his dick. I would lie to my boss about why I was late to work, just to be worked over.

It always ended with him taking my body slowly through the ringer. He always took his time, like a chef preparing fine cuisine.

Michael would start by looking me in the eyes, as if that would make my clothes fall to the floor. Most times he was correct, and my clothes did fall—with a little help from him. He was the smooth operator, the one who let his dick do all the speaking for him. Your only chance of having any control over the situation was to not let him whip it out, because once it was out, there was nothing you could do but bend to its will.

I had gotten pretty good at avoiding the dick whip, so he got smarter. Whenever I came over, he would now beat me to the punch by answering the door naked.

It was like he was a spider, and I was trapped. Yes, I could've walked away, but I knew how I would feel when he finished with me. I knew I would have the best orgasm, and everything leading up to it would leave my toes tingling. I didn't want to walk away.

Every time I let him near me, my panties melted away as he led me to his bedroom. It was the same thing every time. I would try to make small talk, as if I could avoid the inevitable: him taking me to new heights.

It wasn't that I didn't enjoy it. The problem was, I enjoyed it too much—his touch, his prowess made me powerless.

He would always order me to get out of my clothes, and I liked it when he ordered me around. It made me hate him and love him; it made me want to follow his every order. I would tell him no as I undressed, and snapped at him as he pushed me on the bed and spread my legs.

He would always dive right in and suck my clit to attention. My back would arch; my body would glide closer to him. He was so good at it—it was so worth it, each time. He would demand that I open my legs, the legs that closed involuntarily as I tried to capture his tongue somehow with my vaginal lips.

With every disobedient move, his voice would deepen as he told me to spread my legs, and not to close them again. I couldn't help it; the feeling I had was so pleasurable and overwhelming. I was trying to make it last and end, all at the same time. I was on the verge, yet not close enough to grab my much-desired orgasm. He knew it, and he took his time tantalizing me. He didn't care if my legs were closing around him—that made him feel powerful; it let him know he was on top of his game. His goal was to make me cum with his tongue first, then make me cum again and again by any means necessary.

He was well on his way to his goal as he spanked me and once again commanded me to expose my clit to him. He wanted me powerless, with no way to control how and when I came. I wanted to pump; he wanted me to just take it—and I took it.

The explosion would always start at the tip of his tongue and travel down my thighs into my legs and toes.

That beautiful, sought-after feeling would find its way back up past my hips and into my stomach. It traveled up through my breasts, where my nipples were already hard peaks.

It made my hands gravitate to them and twist them. I needed to cum; I wanted to cum, but he wouldn't let me. He would hold out just enough to make me beg him for more. When my back arched, there was no turning back: it was going to happen, whether he wanted it to or not. My body was on autopilot from that point on, and I was experiencing that fall-off-the-roof feeling. My orgasm would squeeze through his lips that were firmly locked around my clit. Ah, the pressure, the pleasure.

This was the great feeling I had every time, but he was more trouble than the good feelings were worth.

He liked drama. He got off on inviting me over there, knowing his girl was going to call and ask to spend time with him. He also lied about even having a woman. I didn't want to be a part of that world anymore. I was finally able to get him out of my system, and forget about him and his magic moves.

But for his last trick, he hit the send button on his phone. He wanted to send me a picture of what he looked like since he'd been working out.

I agreed to let him send it, only to be surprised moments later by a full frontal assault. I was pleasantly surprised at what I was looking at; it was still long and thick. It was still tasty looking, and it looked like it still wanted me.

I once again wanted him to be inside of me, and I was about to extend the invitation to welcome him back to the fold between my legs.

I blinked twice . . . smiled . . . then remembered he'd just told me he was talking to me at the grocery store, which meant he sent me a picture he'd already sent to some other woman. He just wanted me to think this picture was especially for me.

Just like that, he's a bastard again!

CLICK!

Every once in a while, even a girl like me enjoys the soft touch.

Sometimes that happens when she least expects it, and from someone she never thought would reach her on a deeper level.

This One Thing He Did

It wasn't something I was used to. It wasn't even something I really liked to do until that night. It made me feel sexy and wanted, like I was the only woman in his world. I'd never had someone take his time making sure I felt good and felt special. His touch was sensual and soft. It was all I could think about, even weeks after it happened. I wanted him to do it again. I wanted him to make me want him with that simple touch, the one where I was forced to take notice because it was such a subtle move. I had no idea the slight touch of his lips against each of my fingertips was a direct line to every trigger inside of my pussy. With every kiss of my fingertip, I wanted him a little more. I wanted to part my legs and allow him to have his way with me. There wasn't a lot of talking; it was more of a sensual silence. I wanted to moan, maybe even sigh, but I didn't want to ruin such a beautiful moment with noise.

This simple move made my clothes want to melt off; it made me want to wrap my legs around him and show him just how much his hand made me wet for him. If he had used his free hand to take a field trip inside of me, he would've found himself swimming inside of my desire, but I couldn't tell him what I was feeling. I was too embarrassed because he wasn't touching my clit; he wasn't sucking and pulling my breasts; and he wasn't pulling me into him and letting me feel the hardness of his dick—the usual signals that let me know a man wanted me. We were in a moving car. I was driving along the highway, and he sat in the passenger's side. He was making me hot, making me want to take him in any way he wanted and anywhere he wanted. I was all in with this man. My panties were a mess with anticipation. Anyone who could use his lips to send electricity through my entire body—just by kissing one finger at a time—definitely had my insides curious and on fire.

We pulled up to his house. I shut off my car and looked at him. He gazed into my eyes and asked if I was ready to go inside.

I was more than ready; I was on fire with anticipation. All because he held my hand.

When someone holds your hand, he's saying he wants you just the way you are.

Think about every time you see a couple walking down the street hand in hand. There is no mistaking how they feel about each other.

A kiss can mean many things. It can mean you're two friends saying hello or goodbye, you're lovers, or you're in love.

But a kiss is over in a matter of seconds. With a hand hold, you're locked in; there is no denying there is something special between the two of you.

There is no denying the intimacy you two share. The feelings are shared without anyone ever uttering a word.

When he held my hand, I felt everything he was feeling. I understood how desperate he was to be close to me. There was no way I could get away from him. He had me where he wanted me: in his grasp, where he could pull me in close to him. Here he could hold me in his chest, kiss me, and caress me. But there was one thing I was sure of: he didn't want to let me go.

This one thing he did—one thing that was more special than making love to me—was hold my hand.

He held my hand as we sat on his couch.

He held my hand as he wrapped his arms around me from behind.

I'd never felt so safe and so loved—all because he held my hand.

Sometimes sexual attraction isn't about the sex. It's about taking a chance, crossing the line, and putting your heart in the hands of another. It's about taking a step back and allowing yourself to feel with your soul.

Unsealed with a Kiss

It happened a few weeks ago. I still can't stop thinking about it; thinking about him.

This was eight years in the making. I had an attraction to him the first moment I met him.

Well, I'm not sure if it was attraction or if I just thought he looked good and was very doable. I wondered if he was thinking about me in the same way. That thing that happened between us was unexpected and shocking. One minute I was standing there a little tipsy, the next minute— well, let's just say I was tipping over.

There was an attraction so strong I wondered how we had resisted for so long. This night we hovered in each other's breath but were barely breathing. I knew I wanted him to touch me in all of my naughty places.

He was telling me how much he liked me, how great of a woman I was, and how much he wanted to be with me. This was a conversation we'd had before, oddly enough, when he was drunk. It was like he could reach out to me when the liquid courage was influencing his actions. I didn't try to silence him or change his mind about anything he was saying. This was our shot at making something happen, so I needed to keep my mouth shut and let him do his thing. He moved closer to me as he spoke. I held out my arms to embrace him. His face was so close to mine. His lips were right there; all I had to do was move in a little closer. I decided to give it a try.

At first it was slow and hesitant. It was as if we were considering if we really wanted to take that step. It was almost like something out of a romantic comedy, the way our lips lightly touched. My lips gently pulled on his top lip; he kind of pulled away, and I let him. It was too much, too fast, and I knew it. I wanted him more than I thought I did. I thought I was merely attracted to him. I was wrong; I was thirsty for him. All the years of suppressing any type of feelings I had for him were about to pour out of me. I was getting hot all over, even though it was breezy and there was a chill in the air.

I wanted him to come for me, take me up in his arms, and kiss me with the passion I was feeling at that very moment. I needed another chance to be close to him. He kept telling me his feelings, making me drunk with emotion. I wanted him more; my body wanted him, and it had enough of waiting for what it wanted. This was uncharted territory for us, yet the few moments I'd spent in his arms during our brief kiss felt so natural. His lips felt like they were a perfect match with mine. I didn't want to release them.

I couldn't explain what was happening between us. It was as if I were outside of my body at the time.

This time he started kissing me. Our kiss felt desperate, like we were afraid one of us would disappear if we stopped. This kiss was like we were long time lovers separated by thousands of miles and dozens of years, and we didn't want to waste any time using our tongues to speak. I stopped fighting our energy and gave in for a few minutes. In those moments, I felt like I belonged to him and he had complete control over my soul and my heart, which was beating rather fast.

His hands found their way inside of my pants. I felt one hand cupping each of my cheeks. I knew I should back away, and I'm pretty sure I tried, but it didn't work. I found myself still locked in an embrace with a man I'd been secretly longing for.

He wanted to put his hands inside of me, and I wanted that too, but I had to try to resist because we both had "situations."

I broke away from him, but only for a few seconds. I knew I didn't have much time with him. I was only in town for a few days. Before I could catch my breath, we were back at it like horny teenagers.

I had to go—we'd been making out for over an hour. I was late picking up my friend, but I didn't want to leave him.

We got in my car because I was worried he was too drunk to drive. I took him with me to pick up and drop off that friend, and to buy more time because I wasn't ready to say goodnight yet. I wanted him to do more than kiss me: I wanted him to take off my clothes and kiss and lick my naked body. None of that was going to happen in a parking lot.

We needed to go somewhere to get our frustrations out and finally quench the fire that had been brewing for more than half a decade.

He kept asking me to look at him while I was driving—as if he forgot I was going 70 miles an hour down a highway—but my heart was racing thirty times that fast. I wanted to look at him and kiss him and hold him and do things I only dreamed of doing to him. Tonight there was a possibility I would be opening myself up to him in the most personal of ways.

We pulled into his driveway. I didn't know what to expect at this point; I just knew after tonight our relationship was going to be different, no matter what.

He'd asked me what we were going to do and how we were going to do it. I just didn't know, which is what I told him. I told him whatever happened, it had to be natural. We walked into his house, and I wanted to run because I was so afraid of changing our relationship from something that was good and cordial to something complicated and potentially messy.

There was no more time to think about that since we were now inside of his home.

He asked if I wanted to watch a movie or something, because that question was always the precursor to anything and everything. I said yes, but I knew we weren't going to be watching anything since he had my mouth covered with his as I responded.

I was so swept up, I lost my balance—but he didn't let me fall. He held me tighter, steadying me close to his chest. I loved this man's power and strength. He didn't miss a beat with the kissing. Our lips were fully engaged; his hands were working their way over my body. He pulled me close to him by my booty; it made me moan a little because I could feel he was ready to go. Now that we were on his territory, he was more aggressive with his behavior. My protests didn't mean as much as they did when we were out in the open.

Now it was about getting down to business, and I loved his business side. He pulled me closer. He ran his fingers through my short textured hair, and he kept my mouth occupied so I couldn't . . . wouldn't protest.

He let me go for a few moments, but I felt like I was under some type of spell because as soon as he released me, I took off my shoes and glasses. I was going to take off my leggings, but there was no need—he pushed me down onto the couch and pulled them off of me.

All night, he kept saying he wanted to eat my pussy. All night, I kept saying no. But now that there was no barrier in his way and his face was so close to the promise land, I was changing my mind about the night full of Nos.

There was no more time to think: he was there, but I didn't feel the contact. I looked up, and he was looking at me. He came up and kissed me deeply again, making me question my sanity and my relationship with my own man.

I didn't have enough room in my brain to continue to care about that because he had moved back down to the place he promised to lick. I felt his tongue and instantly became nervous again. This was a man I'd known for eight years. Eight years and we'd never kissed, until tonight. Now he was seeing inside of me, drinking me. My nerves subsided quickly after his tongue found its rhythm. I no longer worried about what was going to happen next between us. The only important thing was what was going to happen in the next few minutes. Was he going to make me cum?

He said he was good at it; he said he was nasty with it and he was all of that. I was wet, and he was mopping it all up and making it wet again.

He spread my thighs and put his tongue deep inside of my pussy. It made me jump a little. I didn't have a place to move to; I was just in place, taking the pleasure.

He let his fingers take the place of his tongue, while his tongue licked my clit.

He was going to make me cum. I felt the tingling in my toes. He straightened my legs and rocked my body under his tongue. It was like being with a human vibrator.

I screamed his name and told him not to stop. He licked more vigorously, knowing it was going to make me give him what he wanted. He grabbed the pressure point in my inner thigh again. It heightened every feeling I had down there. He was rough and gentle as he squeezed and licked. He released my legs to put his fingers back inside of me. The buildup was amazing; his hands were just as magical as his tongue.

He knew where to place them to intensify the feelings: he pressed down on the top of my pelvis. It was like he concentrated all the sensation into one little core. That core led to my clit, where his tongue continued to draw moans, screams, and wiggles out of me.

Then, all of a sudden, it just happened: I came with a force that made me close my knees around his head.

He rose, and his mouth met mine. I could taste myself on him. I licked his lips, trying to suck all of me off of him. I wanted to take him all the way in me. I wanted to lick him, taste him, swallow him . . . I just wanted him.

He stopped and lay down. He pulled me to him and wrapped his arms around me.

I normally enjoyed the tussling of good sex after a lick down like that, but him holding me so close to his body, so tight, felt better. He didn't want anything else from me; he just wanted me, and wanted me to be satisfied. He kept kissing me with such fervor; it was as though he thought kissing kept us frozen in time. I didn't want it to end either, but the sun was starting to come up and we needed to sleep, at least for a few minutes.

When we got up the next morning, I felt weird for crossing that line with my friend . . . but I was so happy I did.

I was scared he was going to blame it on the alcohol, but he greeted me with kisses. He pulled me to sit down to his lap, and held me as he kissed me again.

I was a little worried about whether I had morning breath or whether he had morning breath, but it was too late for that; our tongues were already intertwined.

I hadn't kissed this much since I was a teenager, but I liked it more because it was him. He had awakened something in me that I'd suppressed for years: the innocence of making out. We cuddled on the couch. My back was to him and his arms were wrapped around me again. I didn't want to move. Our hands were clasped; it was like we were meant to be together, like our spirits were finally joining the way they were supposed to.

I drove him back to his car. I didn't want to leave him but I had to—real life was calling us both.

Imagine being taken to new heights over and over again.

Just when you thought you hit your peak on the sexual experience scale, you're pushed to new limits beyond the other side.

The Other Side: Part 3

I felt like I was in a dream world. All inhibitions were shed; everything was instinct and intuition now.

No one said, "Switch"; someone else would just touch you. Someone else would kiss your mouth, and someone else would suck on you. I felt like I was the center of attention, since this was my present. I was on my knees with a dick in my mouth and a tongue in my pussy. It could've been a man's tongue; it could've been a woman's.

Someone sticking his or her tongue inside of me made me want the dark, luscious dick that was in my mouth.

I'm not bragging, but I have skills in that department—I knew how to wrap my tongue around him and draw him in like a vacuum. I was gentle but firm. I could hear him moan with pleasure. No, it wasn't my man I was sucking on at that time—he was watching me from the sidelines with a satisfied look on his face.

The man in front of me now wanted to know what I felt like on the inside. He pulled away from me and touched me to turn me around. I was on my back when I felt lips on my right and left breasts simultaneously.

My mouth was open, but I could barely make a sound because I was too overwhelmed with pleasure.

This man was putting everything he had inside of me. My nipples are the most sensitive part of my body, so having two people dining on my favorite body parts made my toes curl. Finally, my man stepped up to the plate took over where the dark knight left off. I was so wet, and I wanted him—I didn't want anyone else at that moment—everyone else could be voyeurs. I told him I wanted to be on top; I wanted him to reach my nipples; I wanted him to bite me.

I looked around the room. Everyone was going at it hardcore, and the more people moaned, the more intense my feelings were.

There may have been music, but there may not have been—the sounds of humping and heat drowned out any other noise.

Someone popped. It was one of the guys; I heard the growl. I wanted to hear that sound from my man.

I rode him harder, rotating my hips around his dick. I knew he was close.

I bent down and kissed his nipples while my ass continued to slam against him. He liked it like that.

It was quiet in the room; that's when I noticed we were the only ones still going. Knowing everyone was watching just energized me. I sat up to showcase my bouncing double Ds. The third guy came up behind me and cupped them. He kissed my neck. Ahh, I could feel the juices dripping out of me; it was a wet mess.

My pussy was singing. You could hear it making what I refer to as the sloshing sound.

Have you ever felt so good that you didn't want that feeling to end? That's how I felt at that very moment.

The whole evening swirled around in my head. The liquor, the weed, and the loving all came down to this one moment: my final orgasm of the night, with all eyes on me. I was going to put on one hell of a show.

I leaned back into the unknown hands and let him work me over while I worked my man's dick between my tight pussy. I could hear the sounds my wetness was making; I could hear the others in the room damn near cheering me on. That part could've been in my head, but whatever I was hearing made me go harder and deeper. I felt my breathing deepen; my heart was beating so fast and hard. I couldn't hold it in anymore. I sucked in, held my breath, and let out the loudest, energizing, primal yell.

My body shook, then I just collapsed on top of my man. Happy friggin' New Year's.

There are times when a drought ensues; those are very trying times. Just like the ground needs to be watered, so does a woman's delicate flower. However, sometimes things don't go according to plan, and you end up wandering through a dickless desert.

The person who finally quenches that thirst is usually in for one hell of a ride.

Reunited

We walked into the hotel room, wrapped our arms around each other, and said a quiet hello as our lips met.

I was in the arms of my kryptonite, Dedrick. I was instantly ready to go, simply because his body pressed into mine. It had been too long since I'd seen him and too long since I'd felt all of his strength forcing my legs apart.

I knew he felt the same way. I could feel it, I could sense it; it was about to be on.

My hands were on the way down below his waist. I couldn't stand being in the same room with him and not have him inside of me. I had been anxious for this evening to arrive—"giddy" would better describe this feeling.

All I could think about was our numerous encounters over the past decade and a half, each and every one ending in pure pleasure. He had never let me down.

I had visions of him demanding I remove my clothes as he stripped down. I knew we would barely be able to get into the room before we'd begin to devour each other, right there on the floor.

I figured he'd push me down on the bed and kiss me lightly but passionately, the way he always did. My body would respond as it always did—with ample amounts of sweetness just for him. I was ready to play out my imagination in those moments following our hello hug, but that wouldn't be the case.

Dedrick was going to make me wait. He would not be rushed, no matter how I pouted or tried to persuade him.

I think he took a little satisfaction in knowing I was so hungry for him, and knowing he was going to let me starve for a little bit longer.

The hard part was over; I had him in the room with me. I knew if I needed to take drastic measures, I would do what needed to be done. I would disrobe and straddle my kryptonite, making him a little weak in the knees.

For now I would wait—wait until he gave me the green light to cum.

We were catching up like long lost lovers separated by distance and time. While I enjoyed listening to every word escaping from his beautiful lips, it was prolonging what I really wanted: him between my legs.

We had dinner, watched basketball, and just laughed, drinking in each other's sexiness. We also had a few drinks and smoked a little something—for old time's sake. I was growing impatient; I wanted him more than he could imagine at that moment. I walked to the bathroom to take off my pants, revealing my purple lace boy shorts.

I wanted to walk back in so he could see how good my behind looked. It was still round, still firm, and still very appetizing.

I needed to get this party started before a sista girl fell asleep. We were both older, and falling asleep was now an involuntary action—so yes, I was worried.

I sauntered over to the couch and sat a bit suggestively. I didn't want him to think I was as pressed as I was to open up to him.

I sat so that one leg was on the couch and the other was on the floor, leaving just enough space for him to play with whatever he wanted down there.

I tried to act like I wasn't watching him as I willed him to touch me, but I knew he got the hint when he began rubbing the thigh that was on the couch. I sighed within myself, happy the show was about to begin.

As he stroked my thigh higher and higher, I inched closer to him.

My pussy and his fingers reacquainted themselves. They moved around inside of me as if they were saying, "Hello, where have you been? We've missed you."

My pussy responded by getting wetter and closing herself around those lovely fingers. They had work to do, and my complete gratification was the end game.

I could hear and feel how juicy I was at that moment. I was feeling famished for him—any part of him, even if it wasn't the part I desired most.

His caress was just the right mix of gentle and pressure. I didn't want to cum like this. The wetness was just the right lubrication to coax the first orgasm out of me. I could feel the pressure building within me. It had been so long since we'd seen each other; the only way I wanted to release was on top of him with his dick deep inside of me.

I worked myself up and down on his digits as if they were an extension of his dick.

I was so turned on at that point I didn't care what was inside of me. He just kept on teasing me, teasing the lust right out of me.

I'm pretty sure he was getting quite a rise out of all that he was doing to me. I couldn't hold out any longer; an explosion was imminent. I could see my breasts rising and falling to the rhythm of my rotating hips. He knew and I knew it was a done deal. I came on his fingers with the ferociousness of a lioness on the hunt.

I felt exhilarated, but I wanted more—I wanted everything he had to give me that night. I wanted to be filled up with him in every way possible.

For the moment, I was happy sitting next to him with our hands and legs touching.

We chilled for what seemed like mere minutes. Thankfully, my kryptonite knows me well enough to know I'm insatiable and I don't need much recovery time once I get going. He was different this time. He was the one who was in charge of this evening. Usually it was me who commanded the night. I always knew what I wanted to do; I knew what I wanted done to me, too, and I always set out to make sure I got it all. Tonight, however, I wasn't running the show: I was the puppet, my kryptonite was the puppet master, and the strings were tied to my legs. He was pulling on those strings right now. I didn't try to fight it—it was like being in a car that was spinning out of control. You don't go against it; you turn into the spin. That's just what I did.

If he would've let me, I would've climbed onto his lap in a hurry. However, those magical fingers, those sexy eyes, and those beautiful lips had me mesmerized.

I was running like a faucet between my legs and silently begging him to plug it with all of that luscious dick he was blessed with.

I savored the good feelings flowing through my toes, my fingertips, and my lower back. I wanted nothing more than to be penetrated.

I knew he was going to make me cum by the way he grazed his hand along my insides. I was open to him in so many ways. I wanted to wrap my legs around his waist. Instead, I closed my thighs around his hand, closed my eyes, and completely surrendered. I know I should've been embarrassed by the show of complete abandon, but I reveled in it until I heard the words I'd been waiting to hear: "Come on."

I tried hard not to seem so eager, but I got up off that couch with haste. I wanted him to take off my clothes, but he would've had to move faster, because I was already hurrying out of my shirt, my panties, and my bra.

The way I envisioned it going started with Dedrick taking me into his arms facing me away from him, my back was pressed into his chest, and my butt resting in his crotch.

I would gently wiggle my hips to help his excitement grow. He would kiss my neck right at the nape. His hands would brush down my breast, lingering long enough to make me squirm. His hands would continue their journey to my waist, my hips, and the inside of my waistband, where he would find a smooth split to part with those now slippery fingers. I would part my legs a little so he could explore me just a bit, long enough for him to see how wet his dick was about to be. I would take those fingers and lick all of me off of him. He would take my shirt over my head and cup my still covered tits while he kissed me. He would keep kissing me until my bra hit the floor. I would help myself out of my panties, making sure to bend over slowly, deliberately, so he could see what he was about to get. If I had any patience, that's how the night would've turned out. Instead, I was naked within 30 seconds.

I was ready to sprawl across the bed so Dedrick could dick me down properly, but again, he reminded me he was running things when he sat his very naked, sexy ass back down on that couch.

I'd forgotten just how thick and beautiful his dick was. It made me salivate and nearly bow to him so I could have it all in my mouth. I wanted to enjoy every lick of the head, and every deep caress. I'd missed his taste, the way he fit in my mouth, and the struggle to take it all in. I shocked myself a little because after waiting and wanting, I was sucking on him like he was one of those sugar daddy suckers—the ones you can only eat using long, lingering draws.

I wanted him in another hole, but I couldn't stop. It didn't help that I knew he was enjoying every time my mouth and tongue slid up and down the very thing that was going to be giving me so much pleasure. I think I was a little drunk with power, but torn—I knew how much he was loving this. I wanted to make him cum in my mouth, but I wanted my pussy to have some fun too. So what's a girl to do?

Answer: she stops so she can get her freak on with her kryptonite. I straddled him on that couch, letting him slide into my wet tightness—and boy, it was tight, I hadn't had it in months. As soon as he was inside, I felt such relief, like taking off a shoe that was too tight. I didn't know if I should move or take solace in this moment; I think I did both. He was moving inside of me, finally. I could feel him hitting my walls. I just wanted to sit there with my eyes closed, taking it all in, because it felt that good.

Memories of our time together were filling my head: the weekend he fucked me raw—yes, I needed ice. There was the time in the back of a rental van; the living room on the floor while my sister slept in the recliner; and the hot tub place. Damn, I missed this man. Being reunited like this, in this moment, erased all of the distance and made time stand still.

Here's the thing: as much as I wanted to be the bump on the log while he poked and prodded my insides, I couldn't help but move around on that chocolate dip stick. His dick intensified the electric pulses traveling through all of the wetness. I wanted more with every rhythmic rock of our bodies. We knew each other's bodies so well, even though it had been a while since he and I had been together. His dick and my pussy were like magnets; they knew how to find each other and sync up, as if no time had passed between them.

There was a slow build up of fire starting deep inside of me—a familiar feeling, a guaranteed feeling with my kryptonite.

Then he did what I love most of all: he grabbed my breasts and began to suck on my nipples while he was still deep inside of me.

First, he began with the left nipple, which made squirm on top of his dick. I knew at that moment I was happy; we were all alone, because he was making sounds come from my mouth that could probably wake the dead.

I couldn't help it, because the nipple was the key to unlocking the kitty. Feeling his lips surround me while his tongue danced around what was now hard, pointed, and very sensitive made me rock back and forth a little faster. It was as if he pushed a button exposing my G-spot. It made me ravenous for him.

I kissed his bald head. I knew I was getting close to an orgasm.

I didn't want to be; I wanted this to last as long as possible. I hadn't sat on his dick in so long; I just wanted to stay there, but my body had other plans. My body wanted to make a creamy mess all over him.

I could feel myself gripping him tighter, and my legs tensed around his lap. I could hear my heart beating faster. I was doing all I could to hold it in, but he was sucking and fucking it out of me. He was now on the right nipple. I scooted up more, bearing down on him. It felt better than good—I didn't know how to express it, other than to say, "Ohhh." I felt like I was hovering, but it was actually me giving up, no longer suppressing my long awaited reward for being such a good girl. I was cumming, and it felt like a balloon being deflated of all of its helium. The pressure being released made me weak and limp, yet energized. He didn't stop; my pulsating pussy fed Dedrick's desire for me. I think we kissed, but I was euphoric—I wasn't sure what was going on anymore, I just felt good.

I knew his lips made it back to my breasts. I kept moving; my hips had a mind of their own. I no longer had control of anything below the waist. It wasn't long before I felt the second wave rushing over my whole body. I tensed up, and when I came down, I shook another one out. He was one of the few people who knew how to navigate my insides without hitting speed bumps. At this point, I'd lost track of how many times he had taken me over the edge this night. We clearly weren't done yet, because he hadn't cum.

I stayed on his lap a dripping wet mess. My kryptonite seemed fine with it. Even though I'd cum twice in that same position, he kept turning the key.

I felt unstable, but so relaxed.

He probably could've gotten me to do anything at that moment since he, in a matter of a few hours, had relieved me and my pussy of five months of a dickless existence. As he sucked and continued to dick down my world, my clit was at the height of sensitivity. Every time he moved, it felt it. Every time I breathed, my clit got a charge. I didn't even realize my pussy was tightening around him again. I heard myself say, "Yes," I couldn't believe I was about to cum again. I whispered in his ear that it was about to happen. I took a deep breath and let it all out. I wanted to faint; I was tapped out, but my muscles were clenched around him. I couldn't let go for a few seconds. Now that's what you call spectacular lovin'.

We took a break because I could no longer feel my legs. I knew it wasn't over, and I wasn't complaining. We had a lot of time to make up for tonight. I guess there was no need to rush at this point.

Dedrick got up and fixed me another drink. He was smiling, and I wondered if he was thinking about how he put a beat down on "his" pussy. (Yes, I said "his"—after what he did to me, he owned it, at least for the night.)

There wasn't much recovery time before he said he wanted to hit it from the back. I was thinking, anything daddy wants, daddy could have. I immediately got wet knowing my kryptonite was about to get back to work on my body.

I assumed the position on my hands and knees. I made my legs spread wide enough to make sure he had no trouble getting to the liquid gold. My booty was out, ripe for the fucking.

I wished I could read his mind at that moment, judging by the way he was brushing his fingers across my back, down my spine, and across my backside. I felt like he was plotting how he was going to make me scream and beg for mercy.

I bent over a little more, subliminally letting him know I was ready for whatever he had to give me.

He said, "Yeah mama," with his smooth voice. It was as if the words were slowly pouring out of his mouth. I was melting from the inside out. Oh, do it to me now, I wanted to say. I was backing up against him, bumping into his erection, wishing it were already inside of me. One breath later, my wish had come true. I was once again feeling his power between my open thighs.

He had me turned toward the mirror. I think I glanced once, just to see what it looked like to have this tall, sexy, chocolate man towering over my very exposed body. Damn, he looked so good—we looked so good. I didn't see much after that. My eyes were closed as I lost myself in every powerful, passionate thrust.

He was so far inside of me it made me jump a little. It was what I liked to call "pleasurable pain." Dedrick knew what he was doing to me, even though he was asking me if I liked it. He knew I liked it; he knew he was my kryptonite; he knew he made me weak. Yes daddy, I thought, but all I could do was nod my head and pant a yes. He spanked my ass. I loved it; it made me work a little harder. The more he pumped, the more I wanted. My body was letting him know, too. I was trying to match his intensity, which wasn't easy because I was buckling. He was relentless.

I knew he was going to drill another orgasm out of me, and I wasn't going to fight it.

He announced he could feel me getting close; he said he could feel the tightening.

I wasn't going to deny it or fight it. I bent into it, meeting his dick head on.

He was in full throttle: he was going all the way in, pulling all the way out, and reentering me over and over again. I got a chance to feel the veracity of his drive every time. Whenever I was close to the edge, he would briefly pull me back, making me work for the gold at the end of the proverbial rainbow.

I swear I heard him ask if there was anyone better than him. I wasn't sure what was happening—I was in a state of pure ecstasy. I said no to what I thought I was answering, hoping I heard him correctly.

He had to know as much as I loved hearing him talk shit while he punished my insides, I couldn't focus on everything being said.

He was the best; he knew me inside and out. Every touch was electrifying, and every pump had a purpose.

He told me what I already knew was inevitable: I was going to cum soon.

It almost sounded like he was smiling as he said it. If I had looked up, I'm sure I would've seen a smirk on his face.

The one thing I knew for sure at that moment was I was desperate for another one.

My breathing was harder. I felt faint, probably because all the blood was rushing from my head to my vagina.

I bent my head into the bed to make sure I was open to everything he was giving. It wasn't long until I ascended to the peak of pleasure.

I was ready to collapse and he still hadn't cum. I knew there was more to come this night, but I was grateful for the break he was allowing me to take.

Believe me, I only needed a short one, because I wanted him all night long. I passed out for who knows how long—cumming like that was exhausting, trust me.

The next thing I remember was him telling me it was time for bed.

Lying in his arms was so relaxing. We were tucked away in our own private world, devoid of worries. It was just us; as close as two people could be.

I allowed myself to relax a little more. I felt safe and unafraid of the closeness with him. We weren't still for long.

Dedrick started rubbing my body lightly, just enough to reignite the flame.

The tiredness dissipated immediately. I was rubbing his dick, making it ready for me.

His touch was making me slippery one more time tonight. My kryptonite was hovering over me in bed. I was definitely up for another romp with this sexy man.

He lifted my legs over his shoulders so he could find his way back to the sweetness he'd been taking in all night.

I wanted him to feel as good as I did, being relieved of so much pressure.

He slid right inside of me. Every stroke felt like a link to my G-spot; his dick pushed on it. The higher my legs went, the more intense the pleasure was.

He told me to turn over. I knew this was it; I knew he was going to ram me until he got what he came for: me in submissive mode, and him getting his the way he wanted it, when he wanted it.

Right now, he wanted to watch my ass while he gave it to me again. His hands were gripping my cheeks as if he was steadying himself. Our movements were quicker, feverishly fast. It was definitely primal. I didn't mind that he was dominating me; he'd earned that right after tonight's performance.

Now he was about to get his reward. I could tell he was close: his breaths were deeper, not quite a growl but very throaty. I couldn't help but smile. I felt good knowing he felt good. He gave it to me harder and harder. I was clenching the sheets, trying to hang on to my balance, until I felt him tense up and explode all over me.

After we cleaned up our mess, it was back in his arms to sleep completely satisfied. When we woke up, I felt rejuvenated, content, and in denial. As the bewitching hour approached, I just lay there, enjoying our final moments, inhaling his scent, wishing I had one more day with him— or a few more hours, at least.

We chatted a little, but there was really no need for words. I felt like we both just wanted to linger in the here and now.

When it was time to say goodbye, I hugged my kryptonite. I didn't want to let go. When I kissed his lips, I didn't want to stop—stopping meant it was time for us to part ways for who knows how long this time.

I would miss my kryptonite the way I always did, but I always kept the memories of the love made close to my heart, in the forefront of my mind, and in the wetness of my walls.

About the Author

A sexual encyclopedia from which her friends are always learning, Zoey Truth has been intriguing and entertaining her friends and lovers over drinks and pillow talk for years. Zoey is living proof that a woman can be a mother, have a successful career, and still tease, taunt, and lust when the lights turn down. A college-educated single mother, at the top of her professional game, Zoey has sought out, and sometimes even stumbled upon, kinky, romantic, and mind-blowing experiences. She views this collection of stories as the skeleton key that can unlock any person's Pandora's box, no matter how hidden. She wants her readers to feel like the eye peering through the peephole, like the ear against the hotel room wall. According to Zoey, "This is only the beginning!"